Henry Green

BLINDNESS

With an Introduction by
Jeremy Treglown

THE HARVILL PRESS
LONDON

First published by J. M. Dent, 1926
Paperback edition published by Harvill,
an imprint of HarperCollins*Publishers* in 1993

This edition first published in 1996 by
The Harvill Press,
84 Thornhill Road,
London N1 1RD

First impression

© The Hon Mrs Henry Yorke 1977
Introduction © Jeremy Treglown 1993

A CIP catalogue record for this book
is available from the British Library

ISBN 1 86046 112 3

Photoset in Linotron Bembo by
Rowland Phototypesetting Ltd, Bury St Edmunds, Suffolk

Printed and bound in Great Britain by
Butler & Tanner Ltd, Frome, Somerset

To my Mother

CONTENTS

INTRODUCTION

Blindness is the first novel of an exceptional writer, and is partly about how the main character manages to become that. "There is more than one way of being blind," Henry Green told a friend who read an early draft[1] – more than one way of being able to see, he meant, too. Like Sophocles' Oedipus, or Gloster in *King Lear*, the blinded John Haye learns that, "It was so easy to see and so hard to feel what was going on, but it was the feeling that mattered."

It is an artist's lesson – one which Henry Green (or Henry Yorke, as he was really called) learned amazingly early, while he was still a teenager. He began *Blindness* at school and continued working on it during a period in France before he went to Oxford, where he finished the book, to the neglect of his studies and against a tide of frustration and unconfidence. No one who reads the story, now, can doubt that Green was bound to have made his way as a writer. But it was a struggle, and his persistence surprised those who had been taken in by his fashionable dandyism, so sharply delineated in John Haye.

On the face of things, "struggle" may seem an exaggeration. Henry Yorke had plenty of advantages. Like Haye, he came from a rich and leisured background and went to Eton ("Noat" in the novel, but in an earlier version, more recognizably "Note"). At school and university, he was friendly with other aspiring writers: Harold Acton, Robert Byron, Brian Howard, Anthony Powell; later, Evelyn Waugh. But these names suggest competition as much as support, and, besides, one of the underlying stories in *Blindness* is Green's need to escape from surroundings with which, however superficially amenable they were, he found himself increasingly at odds: the self-regarding aestheticism of his school contemporaries, the too-easily appreciated beauty of rural England, and the similarly glib literary attractions of what, in the book, he calls "Picture Postcardism".

This last is represented by the melodramatic sub-plot of a drunken, defrocked parson and his battered daughter. Green had been reading George Moore, and *Esther Waters* may have given something to this part of *Blindness*. But just as Haye isn't in the end content with Joan Entwhistle, so the author stopped using books as an imaginative source after *Blindness* appeared in 1926, and went to learn something new for himself by working as a foundryman in the family business. It was as strong a gesture as he could have made to distance himself from Oxford and all that it represented. Other people whom he knew (John Betjeman among them) left Magdalen degreeless, but not so as to live in a working man's lodging-house in Birmingham.

In *Blindness*, the move is both anticipated and also – as was typical of Green – made fun of, when John Haye assumes a social conscience as a way of trying to seduce Joan. Henry Green wasn't George Orwell, and *Blindness* doesn't take Haye's anxieties about ordinary people over-seriously ("God, the boredom of this", the young idealist thinks, as Joan tells him about her pet chicks and mouse). But not all of Haye's attitudes are poses. Stuck in the family's country home, he reflects that, "The life of the century was in the towns, he had meant to go there to write books, and now he was imprisoned in a rudimentary part of life." By the last chapter, he and his stepmother have moved to London.

John's resistance to his stepmother's rural world links the book to the modernist climate in which it appeared, but is also the source of a traditional vein of comedy: a close, affectionate satire on upper-class English life which reminds one of Saki, and was to mark all of Henry Green's in other ways disparate novels. Emily Haye is a horsewoman, as was the author's own mother, whose voice is recognizable in the book. If Mrs Haye reads, it is about hunting ("This book was interestin', she had never known that the Bolton had distemper in '08 and mange in '09, a most awkward time for them, and the bitch pack had been practically annihilated"). If she writes, she uses an inkstand made from a favourite horse's hoof. All this is tender, as well as unsparing. We come to know Mrs Haye better than she knows herself (it is another of the title's meanings). Her obsessions amuse us, but we are made to understand her fears, too, and to admire her courage when she finally gives up everything in order to go with her blind stepson to the city.

There may have been an element of wish-fulfilment in this for the young Henry Yorke. In the spring of 1925, while he was revising *Blindness*, he spent some time with his mother in Paris, and was rueful about their quarrels there. She and his father weren't great supporters of his writing – they showed a draft of *Blindness* to the adventure novelist, John Buchan, and accepted his advice that the young man's efforts shouldn't be encouraged. As if that weren't dampening enough, the book was rejected by the first publishers Green sent it to, Chatto and Windus. He dismissed them, afterwards, as a "despicable firm", but was thoroughly downcast. "I know of no more trying work than that which I have been doing," he wrote. He was apprehensive about the attitude of his tutor, C. S. Lewis, to his having fallen behind with his college work – "really one is left without much energy after thinking round & round the same wornout old subject day after day." In his discouragement, he burned a play he had been trying to write.

If Lewis wasn't much help, Green had a supportive confidant in another young English don, Nevill Coghill (later well known as a translator of Chaucer, and for his OUDS productions of Shakespeare). Coghill had seen draft after draft of *Blindness*, made detailed suggestions, and told Green how sure he was of his promise as a writer. When Chatto rejected the book, it was Coghill who put him on to Dent's, and through them, to the influential editor Edward Garnett – "a huge old man," as Green later described him, "his buttons undone all over the place, who stared you down with pale eyes behind deep spectacles and whose white hair was combed over his forehead in a fringe – a pale-faced, menacing, wordless object, immeasurably tall." Garnett recognized the book's promise of genius, and met the author to discuss it in December, 1925. On Garnett's advice, Green again re-wrote the last chapter. Dent published *Blindness* the following year. Evelyn Waugh (then writing his own first novel) said, "It is extraordinary to me that anyone of our generation could have written so fine a book."

It had been through several titles, including "Young and Old" and "Progression". They were the result of more than youthful uncertainty. Like John Haye, who insists on calling Joan "June", Henry Green / Henry Yorke was perturbed by names, not least his own: at Eton, he appeared in the school magazine as Henry Michaels; on the typescript of *Blindness*, as Henry Browne. In his autobiography, *Pack My Bag*, published in 1940, there is a typically enigmatic, suggestive passage about anonymity, in which he also seems to half-remember his first novel: "When I think of someone I see their face or something about them, it may be their hands, and often have difficulty in putting names to faces. Names distract, nicknames are too easy and if leaving both out . . . makes a book look blind then that to my mind is no disadvantage." A blind book would be a book that couldn't read you, and in Henry Green, more than in most writers, there is a deep argument going on between self-revelation and concealment. Much of his fiction was at some recognizable level autobiographical – was "true", as he told his later editor, John Lehmann about his war-stories. But he wouldn't let his publishers distribute biographical information about him, and turned his back on photographers.

Blindness takes part in this quarrel. In letters to the young author, Nevill Coghill would ask questions about John Haye as an intimate, yet unintrusive way of getting to know Henry Yorke. But they were not the same person, any more than Haye at the end of the book is the same as at the beginning. Perhaps a condition of Henry Green's imaginative freedom was a belief that in some sense he could remain unknown: that his books were blind, or would be read in the dark.

In his great novel, *Loving*, one of the most vivid scenes is centred on blind man's buff – the game in which you have to feel people to tell who they are. John Haye's plight in *Blindness* is a similar metaphor. Among other things, it enables him to hear those around him better, and not only to hear their words but their thoughts. Eudora Welty wrote that Henry Green turned what people say "into the fantasy of what they are telling each other, at the same time calling up out of their mouths their vital spirit"[2]. John Holloway put the point slightly differently, in making a comparison between *Blindness* and the work of John Cowper Powys: "What dominates is a sense of the individual's deeper consciousness, direct and raw, meandering into shape, created out of memory floating and flooding experience, formative even when disparaged; and of consciousness emerging into conversations."[3] This is particularly true of the nanny's affectionate, muddled thoughts, through which we learn not only about her, but about much of what is going on in the house. Some of the book's prodigiousness lies in this early, skilled exploration of new means of conveying narrative and situation: John Haye's schoolboy diary; the letters with which each section ends; the flow between Haye's thoughts and those of the others around him.

From the beginning, Green was an experimenter, and a hard-working one. It is easy to be taken in by the pretence of carelessness. In *Pack My Bag*, he describes his time at Oxford as if he did little there but get drunk and go to the movies. But his notes to Coghill, both when he was an undergraduate and later, are full of news about the stylistic techniques he is trying out, and more than once he says that they can't meet because he wants to get on with his writing. Such commitment and such audacity in a writer of little experience were bound to produce flaws, and neither Green himself nor some of his early readers were completely satisfied with *Blindness*. Even the intensely devoted Coghill passed on objections raised by relations of his who read the book in draft at their family home in County Cork during the summer of 1925:

> Alas they think it difficult, depressing, ungrammatical (!!) carelessly written !!! This so infuriates me that I shout at them, telling them it is a work of undying genius and that they are too crapulous to understand it. To which they reply 'Ah, but I like a good story.' Poor Henry. I am so sorry. But I am sure that your way of writing is a very good way and is right for you . . . and I am also quite unhesitatingly certain that your next book will be so much better that no one will be able to ignore or deride it. And I am only afraid that you will take an unreasoning prejudice against your First-Born, (which I shall have to keep safely from your infanticidal rage) though it is good. It is good.

It was to this letter that Green drily answered that there was more than one way of being blind.

Different readers may have different reservations: particularly, today, about the way Joan is characterized, and the implication that she quite likes her father beating her up ("Her fingers crept to the scar upon her cheek, it had been wonderful that night. You felt a slave, a beaten slave.") To the literal-minded, Haye's accident may also seem unconvincing. But not all such implausibilities are the result of oversight. Even in his mature work, Green often decided against tidying up his writing too much, realizing that touches of what painters call loose handling were needed to set off the rest. In this way he could sometimes allow himself a traditional kind of accomplishment which must have made even John Buchan wonder about his dismissal of *Blindness*. There is the subtlety with which Green suggests the servants' feelings over the Hayes' departure, for example, when William neglects to wind up the clock. Or there are those bravura passages that are characteristic of all Green's work, such as when John remembers fishing:

> The boat floated gently too, a bird sang and then was silent, and he would watch the jaunty fly, watch for the white, greedy mouth that would come up, for the swirl when he would flick lightly, and the fight, with another panting, gleaming fish to be mired in struggles on the muddy floor of the boat . . . The day would draw away as if sucked down in the east . . . A kingfisher might shoot out to dart down the river, a guilty thing in colours.

Fortunately, whatever Buchan thought, Henry Green knew he was a writer. V. S. Pritchett later said he was "the most luminous novelist of the Thirties and Forties – as *Blindness* foretold – and truly seminal". His importance is that of an artist who always went his own way. At the time, Edward Garnett told him he hoped that his next book would be "a most amusing novel called 'The Family Relatives' . . . One with a kindly, satirical view of the activities of the whole tribe". The author's response was to write *Living* and the rest of his nine novels, in which amusement and domestic satire are often present, but where, always trying something new, he went on exploring the unique vision first opened up by *Blindness*.

November 1992   J. T.

[1] I am grateful to Sebastian Yorke, the Hogarth Press and the Provost and Fellows of Eton College for allowing me access to unpublished manuscripts, letters and other materials concerning Henry Green.
[2] "Henry Green" Novelist of the Imagination" (1961), reprinted in *The Eye of the Story: Selected Essays and Reviews*.
[3] *The Times Higher Education Supplement*, 26 August, 1977.

BLINDNESS

Part One

CATERPILLAR

Laugh

Diary of John Haye, Secretary to the Noat Art Society, and in J. W. P.'s House at the Public School of Noat.

6 July (about)

It has only just struck me that a kind of informal diary would be rather fun. No driving as to putting down something every day, just a sort of pipe to draw off the swamp water. It has rained all the past week. We went to Henley yesterday and it was wretched: B. G. going off to Phyllis Court and leaving me with Jonson, an insufferable bore who means very well and consequently makes things much worse. Seymour went with Dore who was dressed in what would be bad form at Monte, and at Henley . . . Had a row with Seymour, and refused to be seen with Dore.

Wonderful T. Carlyle's letters are, and his wife's too. One can always tell them at a glance. She is the best letter writer there has ever been, I am told by a modern authority. I should think T. C. runs this pretty fine, his explosive style going well into letters.

9 July

Two people in my absence just had a water fight in my room, which enraged me.

The usual question asked, "Why not in anyone else's room?" and of course no answer: however, felt better after calling Brimston an animated cabbage. His retort was, "Oh, cutting!" . . .

Seymour, B. G. and I were seriously discussing the

3

production of a revue here next term, as they do at the universities, but as Seymour said, the difficulties were insuperable, too many old men to surmount.

Walk with Seymour to-day, who was very charming. Fell in love with a transparent tortoiseshell cigarette case for three guineas, very cheap I thought. He keeps his band of satellites in very good order. When he told them to leave the School Shop they did. They positively worship him. He is an extraordinary creature, I don't believe he could get on without them: keeping them as some people keep a dog, to let off steam at. A rift between Harington Brown and Seymour, very amusing to watch: H. B. much the same as Seymour but lacks his charm. Seymour furious because H. B. has brought out a bad magazine called *The Shop Window*. Seymour thinks it is a challenge to his precious *Noat Lights*. If it is one it is a failure.

Dicky Maitland, who used to try and teach me science, has been writing to the Adjer to say that my Volunteer's uniform is always untidy; the Adjer says he has had several notes: did you ever hear such cheek? But then the poor man is a military maniac.

As a matter of fact I ought to look quite well tomorrow on the occasion of the Yearly Inspection, as my tunic is nothing but oil stains, and everything else is sketchy and insecure.

J. W. P. told me last night that I was a person who wanted to fail at Noat and who thought (and only he knew how mistakenly) that he was going to be a success in after-life. A typically House-masterish thing to say. But then he was in a bad temper.

Later. – Have just announced that I go to the dentist to-morrow so shan't be able to play in the House match that afternoon: frenzy; "I call that rather a shame," etc. Isn't it funny what a good player one becomes on a sudden?

The dentist to-morrow will be the third time he has tried to kill a nerve, and it isn't nearly dead now, but still fairly active.

Tremendous excitement over Hutchinson's coming novel, everyone trying to get a first edition.

Thursday

Corps Inspection: all went well.

Afterwards I went up to the dentist, and in the train met Mayo who is leaving early. Had a long talk mainly about Seymour and Co. As might be expected he did not like him, but what was more to the point, produced a most interesting reason and unanswerable to a person who holds views like his. Firstly, then, he has no use for a person who is no good at anything. He tolerates the clever scholar, he tolerates the half-wit athlete, but since he cannot see that any of us are remotely even one of these, he cannot bear us as a set.

What adds fuel to his fire is a person who glories in his eccentricity, which of course is true of all of us, in that we glory in ourselves. And of course the inevitable immorality touched on, which is always connected with eccentricities.

B. G. of course he merely regards as really and actively evil, and I don't blame him as he does not know B. G., whose appearance is well calculated to sow the seeds of doubt and dislike in any righteous person. Furthermore, he can't see what good any of us are going to do in after-life. He said that he was going into the army, he trumpeted that, and then because we were alone together he put me out of the argument by saying that I should be a future financier.

I could not answer him, there was nothing further to say, but in the course of the running fire that we kept up afterwards just to show that there was no ill-feeling, he actually said that Seymour went up in his estimation because he had won his House hundred yards. Extraordinary! Very

5

interesting, and, of course, a view which is almost incredible to me, in fact a great eye-opener.

Had to return in a hurry from the dentist who has given up trying to kill the nerve in my tooth. He prophesied what he called a "sting" in it to-night: he under-estimated it considerably. It is hurting damnably.

21 July

Am reading a very good book on the Second Empire with Napoleon the Third. It is in the Lytton Strachey style, which after Carlyle's is, I think, the most amusing.

The Volunteers' Camp and all its attendant horrors is getting quite close now: though I could get off whenever I wanted to with my hammer-toes, but I want to go just for once.

22 July

Bell's, across the way, have bought as many as seven hunting-horns. Each possessor blows it unceasingly, just when one wants to read. They don't do it all together, but take it in turns to keep up one forced note. Really, it might be Eton. They can only produce the one note during the whole day.

In addition to this trifling detail, it is "the thing to do" now to throw stones at me as I sit at my window. However, I have just called E. N. a "milch cow," and shall on the first opportunity call D. J. B. a "bovine goat," which generally relieves matters. These epithets have the real authentic Noat Art Society touch, haven't they?

24 July

No Art Society this evening. No one turned up except H. B. who was to have read a paper; he was rather hurt. However, I think it will be all right, he has about as much admiration for the satellites as I have.

Am too tired to do anything but write this. The House

rather alarmed and faintly contemptuous to hear I keep this; they have given me up, I think and hope. Rather a funny thing happened while fielding this afternoon. I had thrown myself down to stop a ball and I saw waving specks in my eyes for two minutes afterwards. I suppose my blood pressure was disturbed.

"For those in danger on the sea" is at the moment being sung by Truin's at House prayers.

26 July

J. W. P. came in last night to say that I had bad reports, everyone saying that I took no trouble, which is not surprising on both sides of the question: says that next term I shall have to do all my work in his study with the half-wits, a song which I have heard before, I think, though it is so encouraging coming at the end of a term's boredom.

Camp at Tidworth will be delightful in this soaking weather.

27 July

Have bought the most gorgeous sun hat for a horse in straw for sixpence, and have painted it in concentric rings. Shall wear it at Camp, and have fixed it up so that it will bend when worn like a very old-fashioned bonnet. In the ear-holes I am going to put violently swearing colours, orange and magenta, in ribbon I got for nothing by being nice to a shopwoman at Bowlay's. Our little John is getting on, isn't he?

The hat is a masterpiece, and being so has, of course, started a violent controversy. Those who consider it merely bounderism, and those who think it amusing, talk very seriously together and stop when I approach, while the faithful come in occasionally to tell me what the others have said.

The most beautiful letter ever written is undoubtedly that of Charlotte Brontë's on her sister Emily's death.

7

No more work till the summer holidays. Have been rel-
egated by the House selection committee to the dud tent
at Camp, which amuses me vastly. Apparently those who
manage the affairs of the tent prefer Bulwer and Maston to
myself; more amusing still. Shall I get elected into the Reading Room next term? Probably not. I think as a matter of
fact they want a mobbing tent which they know I would
not join in, anyhow I shall be much more comfortable as I
am: at any rate that reads better, and sounds so for that
matter.

Apparently I shall get attacked if I wear my straw hat, a
fact I can hardly believe. I have had *the* most heated arguments as to why I should not wear fancy dress; the fact
remains that people are more prim and hidebound there
than here, except that, as far as I can see, all and sundry
combine to be rude to other schools.

A sing-song in the Hall to-night, to which everyone but
myself has gone: didn't go for two reasons; first, because
the cinema part of it was certain to be lamentable; secondly,
Fryer irks me when he sings songs, and the applause he
gets, for no other reason than that he is everything at games,
and so is profitable to applaud, maddens me.

What is bad is that this school tends to turn the really
clever into people who pretend for all they are worth to be
the mediocrities which are the personification of the splendid manhood phrase. And in the end these poor people
succeed and lose all the brains they ever had, which is dis-
tressing, particularly for me who could do with a few more.

Sing-song apparently a great success. There is an auction
going on now, everything that has been handed down
through the ages is being resold. I suppose some pictures

have seen about forty auctions: the commonest are Thorburn's petrified partridges, or worse still, those most weird and antiquated pictures of horse-racing, the horse's neck being the length of its body.

Social ostracism which I am experiencing now for the first time for many terms is really incredibly funny. It begins with a studied vagueness when you address anyone, which means that he is frightened at being seen talking to you: it goes on, in direct ratio to the number of jaws they have about you, to a studied rudeness, and the lower and younger you are the more your room is mobbed. And then the whole thing blows over you on to some other unfortunate.

I suppose I have been rather tiresome lately, but all except T. D. and possibly E. N. are so distressingly the athletic type, who sink their whole beings in the school and its affairs, and are blind and almost ignorant of any world outside their own.

31 July

The last flourish before Camp.

My room is a sight for the gods, piles and stacks of clothing to be packed, a bulging pot-bellied kit-bag filled with changes of clothing for the ten days' horror, everything upside down, and over all the frenzied maid as near suicide as she ever gets: her chief job is to look for lost garments, and as she regards me with the deepest suspicion over a pair of tennis shoes, I am not left long alone. The storm in the Chinese tea-service has died down, and once more I am anchored precariously outside the haven of the barely tolerated.

I hear that the only hotel where one can get a bath in Camp has been put out of bounds, which is delightful. How furious Mamma will be: apparently the reason is that people used to drink there.

Just a scrawl. It has been raining viciously as if with a purpose. At the moment I am lying on what is affectionately known as a "palliarse." Underneath is deal planking. Underneath that is a torrent as we are on a hill and the accumulated effects of two days' rain are flowing beneath. Above is a bell tent, long since condemned by the army authorities as unsound, so that the cloudburst which is pouring from Heaven penetrates freely. There is one spot under which lies Brown, the world's greatest grouser, and it is appropriately threadbare. He was foolish enough to put soap on it; we had told him that if you soaped a bit of cloth it became waterproof, and now soapsuds drip down on to his face. We have also told him that his grousing is intolerable, and will be dealt with unless he suppresses it, so that he lies in a misery too deep for words, and is the only thing that keeps us happy.

There are, of course, rumours about our going home on account of the wet, but such a good thing could not possibly happen.

The food and the smell of grease in the eating tent are both very foul. The smell I was warned against by an old campaigner. Thank God my turn has not yet come for washing up, but I shall have to do it to-morrow. They are thinking themselves the most awful devils in the next tent with a bottle of port; perhaps if I had one I should feel one too.

The village fête here yesterday, and after a three forty-five awakening, *reveille* or whatever you like to call it, at Tidworth, I had to run about here when I arrived and be officious to all and sundry. An awful thing happened. It was towards the end when I was so tired I could hardly see. Mamma told me to go and find the young lady who ran the Clock Golf Competition and tell her to send in the names of the prize-winners. The young ladies who ran things were all surprisingly alike, disastrously so, and there were many of them. I went up to a girl I was sure had run the Clock Golf, and I asked her if she had done so. No answer. Again I asked, and again no answer. Somehow I felt only more sure from her silence that she had run it, so I asked her yet again, and more eagerly. There was no answer, but there came a blush like a banner which rallied all her friends to her, to protect her from the depredations of this young man. After that I hid myself in the house. I know what the neighbourhood will make of my reputation now. Mamma laughed; I have never heard her laugh so much before.

I have got the most vile and horrid "bedabbly" cold – Carlyle again. Had one or two highbrow talks with Seymour in a small canteen with two cubic feet air-space for each savage human, which was rather wonderful.

29 August

I fished to-day and "killed" two tiddlers, one was a minnow, and such a small one at that that I thought it too infinitesimal even for the stable cat. That was a record broken, if in the wrong direction.

Mamma to-night on religion. What effect it had, and how far it went, at Noat? They are effectively stifling mine.

During dinner I saw a man run across the bottom of the garden, so when it was over I took the dogs, and with an eye to theatrical effect I put the bulldog on a leash, and led him snorting, pulling, panting and roaring round the garden. He made just the noise, on a minor scale, that one is led to believe a dragon made. William waited with Father's revolver loaded with blank, awaiting a scream from me if I was attacked. He looked too ludicrous, with a paternal smile on his face.

To my mind there is nothing so thrilling as the rushing, hungry rise the chub ~~have~~ here; it makes me tingle even now to think of it, and the more spectators on the bank watching, after you have hooked your fish, the better.

At the present Mamma is in a great state over someone on the Town Council of Norbury. After swearing me to secrecy she told me all about it, and I have forgotten. But the main thing is that she has her suspicions only and no proof, but that, of course, only makes her more sure. But she had a splendid speech in the middle about dishonesty on town councils when she was at her best. But I wish she would not take these things so seriously. She expects me to too, and when I don't, she says, "Ah! you are too young, John dear."

Mamma not sleeping, so Ruffles, the chow, passed the night in my room, which he disliked intensely, so much so that when he did eventually doze off distrustfully, he had what is a rare thing with him, a nightmare of the most alarming and noisy order. I hope this Town Council business is not really keeping Mamma awake. Probably the wretched devil is quite innocent. It would be quite like Mamma to go up to him and accuse him of it. But then she couldn't.

Caught seven fish yesterday, which wasn't so bad. They were rising well.

Back to the old place again, and very depressed in consequence: however, I am now a full-blown specialist in history, and am allowed to send small boys on errands as I am one of the illustrious first hundred in the school. But the football is going to be awful.

I came back on Wednesday. As usual, nothing is changed in the least: Bell's opposite have discarded their hunting-horns of accursed memory for an accordion and a banjo, just as painful.

What with the accordion and the cold and the noise and the discomfort and Cole, who I am up to in history, this has ceased to be a life and has become a mere existence. However, the outlook is always black at the beginning of the term.

Later. – An excellent meeting of the Art Society: very amusing. There was a grand encounter between Seymour and Harington Brown and B. G.'s unrivalled powers of invective were used with great effect. His face, his voice, everything combines to make him a most formidable opponent in wordy warfare.

1 October

Since all my contemporaries spend all their time in the Senior Reading Room with a newly-acquired gramophone, I am left alone and undisturbed, which is very pleasant. Am feeling much more cheerful now, which I attribute to a cup of hot tea.

Am keeping up all the traditions by being the only person in the school with a greatcoat on. Why is it that when there is the hardest and most bitter frost no one wears a greatcoat here? I think it is so absurd, and get rewarded for my pains by catching reproving glances from the new boys, who, of course, are ultra careful, so much as to say, "You are making an ass of yourself with that coat on."

Seymour and B. G. are going to give *the* most immense and splendiferous leaving party, which is going to be wild fun.

3 October

This morning an outrage: I am eating my morning bun, given to me for that purpose by J. W. P., when my tooth meets a stone, and half of it is broken off clean. Result, an immense jagged cavity which I shall have filled, at J. W. P.'s expense, with platinum, and set with brilliants. I am furious.

Brown, a friend of mine, has hit Billing, who keeps the food shop where you get rat poison, in the stomach so that he crumpled up behind the counter: the best thing that has happened for years.

Billing had apparently hit Brown previously, and had sent him to the Headmaster for being rude, and he, instead of backing Billing up, had asked Brown why he had not hit him back: so when Billing hit Rockfeller to-day, Rockfeller being with Brown, Brown was rude to Billing, who attacked Brown, who laid Billing out. Meanwhile Brown has gone to his House master to ask that Billing's shop may be put out of bounds, and Billing presumably is going to the Headmaster. There will be a fine flare-up.

6 October

Rejoice, O land! My director on seeing my first essay, and a bad one at that, tells me I ought to do well with my writing. What fun it would be if I could write! I see myself as the English Anatole France, a vista of glory . . . superb!

I have fallen hopelessly in love with the ties in Bartlett's window. I shall have to buy them all, even though they are quite outrageous: the most cunning, subtle and violent checks imaginable.

Sunday, 8 October

This morning we had a howling dervish of a missioner who comes once a year. All his ghastly stories were there and his awful metaphors and his incredible requests. In this morning's sermon he asked us to give his mission a vision; last time it was that we should pray for it, and before that, that we should give up our holidays to work there. To-day we were told that even cabbages had visions, and God knows what else. He was upset by our laughing at him and he broke down several times, Chris crowning himself with glory by going out in the middle of the man's discourse clasping a pink handkerchief to his nose which he said was bleeding. Really the pulpit is no place for self-revelation, but I am afraid the man has not learnt it yet.

9 October

Two youths have been insolent to me in the Music Schools. Am I considered the school idiot? If so I am not surprised; any way I was most polite to them – next time measures will be taken. The best way with these people is to ask them their names; it generally shuts them up. I believe my appearance is too weak; I shall have to grow mustachios. I am always the person the lost Asiatic asks his way from, and French come to me as fly to fly-paper, ditto the hysterical matron. Such is fame.

12 October

Guy Denver tells me the following: It is extremely cold, and he and Conway are walking together. Says Conway, "God, I am cold!" Guy: "Then why don't you wear an overcoat?" "Oh! then I should be classed with the John Haye and Ben Gore lot." That is what the fear of popular opinion drives the ordinary Public Schoolboy to; that sort of thing is constantly recurring like the plague.

15 October

This afternoon a delicious six-mile walk with B. G. The weather was perfect, a warm sun and everything misty, with "the distances very distant," as Kipling puts it. Though we did not rock the world with our utterances, it was very enjoyable indeed.

20 October

Greene has ordered several chickens' heads, lights, etc., to be sent up to White, which we hope will be a nice surprise. It is rather a good idea.

Have been painting a portrait of Napoleon, cubist and about three foot square, with B. G., who has got it as a punishment from a new master. He will soon lose that most refreshing originality. Moreover he said that B. G. was not to do anything comic, which showed that he was already beginning to lose it. It just depends how much the others have instilled into him to see his manner of receiving our glaring monstrosity.

New phrase I have invented: "To play Keating's to someone else's beetle." Used with great success on Seymour who is enraged by it.

21 October

This morning, so I am told, Seymour and B. G. dragged a toy tin motor car along the pavement on the end of a string. How I wish I had been there: it is quite unprecedented, and seems to have outraged the dignity of the whole school, which is excellent.

Seymour created another sensation by quoting his own poetry for to-day's saying lesson, which caused much amusement. Everyone who matters athletically now thinks it is the thing to do to know Seymour, which is intensely funny, and into the bargain I feel I get a little reflected glory when I walk with him down the street. The Captain of the Rugger smiled at me the other day. I nearly spat in his face (but of course I really smiled my nicest).

Have written to several artists to ask them to talk to the Society. When we founded it we put in the rules that we must get men down to speak to it; it is the only way of keeping the thing alive. And I think if we can get someone down the Society will recover from its present rather dicky condition.

25 October

Have just had a letter from the biggest swell I wrote to, saying that he will come down to the Society on 14 November.

It really is too splendid: he is the most flaming tip-top swell who has written thousands of books, as well as his drawings, which are very well known indeed. All these people are so nice and encouraging about the Society, which is splendid.

31 October

I am seventeen now – quite aged.

Last night was the gala invitation night of the Society, and was an *immense* success, where I had secretly feared failure.

All those invited came – all the boys, all the masters, and all to-day I have been hearing nothing but how pleased and interested they were. It was on Post-Impressionism, a subject which had the merit of being one which the Society knew more about than anyone else present. B. G. made the most gorgeous speech of pure invective which enthralled everyone. The Society is now positively booming, even T. R. C. having thawed into enthusiasm. I think it is a permanency now.

Fires on alternate nights now, which isn't so very, very bad, and the weather is slowly improving. Extraordinary how the weather affects my spirits. I had a telegram from Mamma who had remembered my birthday, which is splendid, for somehow I hate its being forgotten. She never remembers till Nan reminds her. But the football, it is enough to kill one.

Would you believe it – but J. W. P. gave me a long jaw on the "hopelessness" of my having a bad circulation, because I habitually wore a sweater underneath my waistcoat: it's a filthy habit, I know, but he drives one on to it with his allowance of fires, and then he tries to blame one: it is an outrage.

It is freezing again, bad luck to it.

B. G. and I in the morning went up to Windsor and got some electioneering pamphlets from the Committee Rooms, and have posted them all over Noat, including the Volunteers' Notice Board and the School Office and the Library. Later I put them up all over the House notice boards, which scored a glorious rise out of "those that matter." These people are really too terribly stodgy; they have no sense of humour, though they did faintly appreciate the pamphlet on the maids' door which said that Socialism was bent on doing away with marriage.

This afternoon I had to read fifty pages of mediæval history, which has left my brain reeling and helpless: it is too absurd making one learn all about these fool Goths and Vandals: they ceased to count in practical politics some time ago now, so why revive them?

Have just conceived the idea of having a gallery of all the people I loathe most at Noat to be pasted up on the door of my room, which has been denuded of the rules of the Art Society since I spent a frenzied afternoon changing the room slightly.

Smith, the master, crosses his cheques with a ruler. One comes across something amazing every day here.

This is the coldest day I have ever met at Noat, and a very thick fog thrown in, greatly conducive to misery, but strangely enough I am most cheerful, having written a tale called *Sonny*, which is by far the best I have done so far.

Quite the most wonderful day of my life. It was polling day, so after two o'clock (a saying lesson so we got out early), B. G., Seymour and I went to Strand caparisoned all over with Conservative blue and with enormous posters.

When we reached Strand, we found all the Socialist work-ing-men-God-bless-them drawn up in rows on either side of the street, so we three went down the rows haranguing. We each got into the centre of groups, and expected to be killed at any moment, for there is something about me that makes that type see red. However, they contained them-selves very nicely while we talked nonsense at them.

Then we went to the station and got a cab, and with B. G. on the box and Seymour and I behind we set off, B. G. with posters stuck through his umbrella, and dead white from excitement. We went by the byways shouting and screaming till we came to the top of the High Street. We then turned down this; by this time all of us were worked up and quite mad, and eventually came to the Cross again, where we passed the Socialists who were collected in a meet-ing. They cheered and hooted, and we went round the same way only shorter, and after going down the High Street, turned down towards Noat, where we soon picked up six or so Noatians. With them we returned, some running, with a rattle making a deafening din. We passed the Labour and Socialist meeting on the "Out" road of the railway station, and went over the railway bridge, where we paid off the cab. We then returned in a body past the meeting, which broke up and followed across the cross-roads, pelting us with rolled-up rags, etc. Then at the corner of the road to Noat we formed a meeting. I was terrified at moments, and wildly exhilarated the rest. The meeting lasted twenty minutes, questions being asked the whole time. B. G. did most of the speaking; Seymour and I did a little too. Wood-ville harangued the women; he was very good with them. They had their spokesman, an old labourer, very tub-thumpy, and the whole of this part of the entertainment is a blur. Looking round in the middle of it I saw that all the Conservative men and women were formed up behind us, which was touching. All this time messages were coming from the fellows on the outside that the people there were talking lovingly of murder (on us), and matters did look very nasty at one time, but it worked off. The police came at the end with an inspector and marched us off, I shaking every man's hand that I could see. So we returned shouting madly. It was too wonderful; never to be forgotten.

16 November

I now understand why men were brave in the war; it was because they were afraid of being cowards, that fear overcoming that of death. The crowd in Strand and having to go back into it again and have things thrown at one – it was terrifying at first for so great a coward as myself, but great fun when one got hotted up. The women were by far the worst. One old beldame screamed: "You dirty tykes, you dirty tykes!" continuously.

Later. – Another wonderful time. I went with Seymour up to the market-place of the town of Noat, outside the Town Rooms, and there we had another stormy meeting. I talked a very great deal this time; Bronsill and I went on the whole time to rather an excited crowd. Then he and I were dragged off and put on a balcony where the Press photographed us, and he addressed the crowd and I prompted him and hear-heared, etc. I would have spoken had there been time, but lunch arrived and we departed. It was too wonderful; it is tremendous fun being above a crowd, about 150 this time, and I wasn't a bit nervous. Nor was I terrified when the crowd became nasty again as on the previous day; it is the most exhilarating thing I know – far better than hunting. Meanwhile, a master saw me and J. W. P. knows. What will happen?

17 November

Nothing happened with J. W. P.; he didn't mind, and was vastly amused.

Have written another story all about blood; not impossibly bad but sadly mediocre. If only I could write! But I think I improve. Those terrible, involved sentences of mine are my undoing.

Fox was pleased at my admiring Carlyle.

Harington Brown asked me for an MS for the magazine he is producing: gave him *Sonny*, but don't suppose it will be suitable, though I am sure it has some worth. The thing is only about 1400 words, and when he refuses it I am going to send it up to some London magazine which will take very short stories, and at present I don't know of one.

I rather hope that H. B. won't accept the thing. The ephemerals are always putrescent, and nobody with any sense reads them. There have been about three editions of it so far, one a term.

Have been accepted by H. B., with mixed feelings on my part. However, his thing is a cut above the usual ephemeral and is quite sensible, but there is a sense of degradation attached to appearing in print. But I hope this means that I can write; it's not bad work as I'm only just seventeen. Perhaps it is too good, and I shan't do anything again.

Carlyle's flight to Varennes in his *Revolution* is almost too painful to read, so exciting is it to me. It is all untrue, of course, they did not go half as slow as he would make out, nevertheless it is superb.

Thank God there are only a few more weeks of this football.

★　　★　　★

What a long interval, and what a very little has happened! The holidays were enlivened by two deaths in the village, which much excited Mamma, and one or two scandals in the neighbourhood, which she followed carefully without taking up sides.

The bulldog died, which was very sad; he was such a dear old thing. Mamma was very much upset about that too, in her funny way. She seems to spend more and more time in the village now, and to see less and less people. One comes back here looking forward to the fullness of the place.

We came back yesterday, and I feel absolutely lost without B. G. and Seymour, who have both left. They do make a gap, for we three understood each other, and we ladled out sympathy to each other when life became too black. And now I am alone, in a hornets' nest of rabid foot-ballers.

At the moment I am reading Gogol's *Dead Souls*. His word-pictures are superb: better than Ruskin's or Carlyle's, and his style is so terse and clean-cut, at least it is in the translation, but it shines through that. I am an absolute slave. I shall keep this book for ever by me if I have enough cash to buy it with. He is wonderful.

He is at his best, I think, in description; I have met nothing like it. Almost he ousts Carlyle; not quite, though. He is a poet through and through.

29 January

But surely this is most beautiful:

The trills of a lark fall drop by drop down an unseen aery ladder, and the calls of the cranes, floating by in a long string, like the ringing notes of silver bugles, resound in the void of melodiously vibrating ether.

He is a poet: and his book is in very truth a poem. It is Gogol.

Am reading Winston Churchill's biography of his father, which is very wonderful.

I hardly remember B. G. as having existed now. That doesn't mean to say that I don't answer his letters, but life goes on much the same.

Did I say that I had become the budding author at home? No, I think not. I have written in all three things, so that I am hailed as a Napoleon of literature. Such is fame. I only wish I deserved these eulogies, and must set seriously to work soon. Mrs Conder most of all seems impressed. Talks at tea of nothing but where she can take me to get "copy" – which means Brighton, I suppose; not that horrid things don't happen there, though. But she is the limit. Since Conder died she has blossomed. At least, when he was alive, one could make allowances for her, because he was so foul, but now there is nothing to say. She is so *gay*, so *devilish gay*! But all this is very untrue, unkind and ungrateful. In all she has given me £5 in tips, and a cookery book for Boy Scouts.

In a moment of rash exuberance I bought a cigarette-holder about eight inches long. Have been smoking it all the afternoon. Caused quite a sensation in the middle-class atmosphere of the tea shop *chez* Beryl.

Am delivering an oration to the Arts Society on Japanese Art. I am going to speak it and not read it, which is bravery carried to foolhardiness. But it is good to get a little practice in speaking.

Just been to dinner with the Headmaster. I was put next him and occupied his ear for twenty minutes. In the course of that time I managed to ask for a theatre for the school to act in, and for a school restaurant where one could get a decent British steak with onions, and, if possible, with beer. I also advanced arguments in favour of this. The only thing we agreed on was the sinfulness of having a window open. He listened to it all, which was very good of him.

On Monday I got off my speech on Japanese Art all right, I think, save for the very beginning, which was shaky to a point of collapse. To-morrow I go to tea with Harington Brown. Meanwhile at the tea Dore gave we arranged that the Art Society should give a marionette show. The authorities agreed the next day and gave us the Studio. Someone is busy writing the scenario, about lovers thwarted whose names end in *io*. Then we shall paint scenery. It will be such fun. Of course the figures will be stationary.

The only modern Germans who could paint are Lembach and Boechel.

24 February

Had tea with H. B. I have sent him a story for this term's *Noat Days*. It won't be accepted, I suppose. It is an experiment in short sentences. He read me the libretto of the marionettes as far as he had got, and it really was remarkably good. He is producing it in his ephemeral.

10 March

This morning occurred one of those incidents which render school life at moments unbearable to such as myself. I was raising a spoonful of the watered porridge that they see fit to choke us with, when someone jerked my arm – The puerility of it all, yet a wit which I, for my years, should enjoy according to nature. Of course there was a foul mess, as of one who had vomited, mostly over me. However, it only took an hour or so to regain my equanimity. Incidentally I had a little ink-throwing exhibition in the fool's room. I had always wanted to see the exact effect of throwing a paint brush at the wall to appreciate Ruskin's criticism. It was most interesting.

Later. – What an odious superior fellow I am now! It is my mood to-night. Sometimes I think it is better to be just what one is, and not be everlastingly apologising for oneself in so many words. To be rude when you want to be rude – and how very much nicer it would make you when you wanted to be nice. I am sure it is all a matter of relative thought. You think you are working hard by your standards, and to another man you don't seem to be working at all. Don't you work just as hard as the other really? Because, after all, it is only a mental question. I shall expound this to J. W. P. I have already done so to Gale with rather marked success. It is a very good principle at Noat.

11 March

I wish the world was not so ugly and unhappy. And there is so much cynicism. And why does Science label and ticket everything so that the world is like a shop, with their price on all the articles? There are still a few auction rooms where people bid for what they think most worth while, but they are getting fewer and fewer. And people love money so, and I shall too I expect when I have got out of what our elders tell me is youthful introspection. But why shouldn't one go through something which is so alive and beautiful as that? But they only say, smiling, "Yes; I went through all that once; you will soon get over that." I shall fight for money and ruin others. Down with Science. Romanticism, all spiritual greatness is going. Soon music will be composed by scientific formulæ; painting has been in France, and look how photography has put art back. Oh, for a Carlyle now! Some prophet one could follow.

15 March

Spent a whole afternoon at work on the marionette stage. I carpentered while E. V. C. tinkered up the scenes he has painted. Between us we got through surprisingly little in a surprisingly long time.

25

My story in the new *Noat Days* will appear shortly. I read the proofs of the story at extreme speed and thought I had never read anything worse or feebler. The paltry humour sickened me, though the end did seem to have some kick in it.

19 March

The marionette show becomes more and more hectic. One hardly has time to breathe. There is a performance on Saturday: the day after the day after to-morrow. Nothing done, of course, and the Studio a scene of hysterical budding artists, mad enough in private life, but when under the influence of so strong and so public an emotion surpass themselves in do-nothing-with-the-most-possible-noise-and-trouble.

1 April

The marionette play continues to be an immense pleasure. We give a children's performance to-morrow at three. Answers from mothers pour in: I am afraid it may be too full. How well do little children see? They are so *very* low down when they sit. I think the life of a stage manager must be one of the most trying on this earth.

Good Friday

On a Pretty Woman, "And that infantile fresh air of hers" (from Browning).

"If you take a photograph of a man digging, in my opinion he is sure to look as if he were not digging" (Van Gogh). Have been reading Van Gogh's letters. They are the hardest things I have ever taken on. He is so very much in earnest, and so very difficult to understand. I think I have got a good deal of what he means.

A wonderful postcard from B. G. in Venice:

We are here till Thursday, wondering who has won the Boat Race, the National, the Junior School Quarter-Mile and the Hammersmith Dancing Record.

Read a little Carlyle to a few of the House. What else could it be but incomprehensible to them? "Mad," they called it. Anything of genius is "mad" in a Public School. And rightly so, I suppose.

4 April

One day more to the end of the term. How nice it will be to be back, to start life again for a day or two. The holidays are disgustingly short, though, only three weeks and a bit.

We have just given our third and last performance of the marionette play. It has been a wild success and should, if possible, be repeated. But the light in the summer would be too strong and everyone leaves at the end of next summer, so I don't suppose we shall have enough people to get one up next winter.

Oh, for to-morrow to go quickly!

Holidays: 10 April

Back again to peace, even if it is cotton wool and stagnation, but very pleasant all the same. Am reading George Moore's *Ave* with considerable relish and amusement. He is so very witty.

My reports have come in and are uninteresting: no one very enthusiastic, which is not to be wondered at.

20 April

"Polygamy is a matter of opinion, not of morality." Montague Glass is undoubtedly the greatest comedian of letters. *Potash and Perlmutter* is superb.

At dinner to-night Mamma informed me in one of her rare pronouncements on myself, that I always kept people at arm's length. It sounds an awful thing to write, but I seldom meet anyone who interests me more than myself: my own fault, I suppose.

We have acquired a gramophone, and Strauss' "Last Waltz" has bewitched me. It is such a lovely thing.

NOAT, 4 May

Back to it again: good old Noat, bloody place! Have just seen a book entitled *Up Against it in the Desert*, which sufficiently describes my feelings at the moment.

It is so hot as to make writing impossible as my pen and style testify. I shall play no cricket this term, but will just read. I can get off the cricket on the score of health, which becomes increasingly bad. Last holidays we went from doctor to doctor. They look on one as an animal of a certain species, those people, than which nothing is more irritating.

5 May

The weather continues to be quite lovely. I pass the afternoon watching the cricket, with a book. It is the nicest thing to do I know. This evening I went on the river. What is it that is so attractive in the sound of disturbed water? The contrast of sound to appearance, perhaps. Water looks so like a varnished surface that to see it break up, move and sound in moving is infinitely pleasing. Also it is exhilarating to see an unfortunate upset.

I must work hard at writing. There are all sorts of writers I have never read; Poe, for instance, the master of the suggestive. I think my general reading is fairly good, but I have such an absurd memory.

2 June

Two portraits of me in the Noat Art Society Summer Exhibition. Not very good, but both striking.

★   ★   ★

Many things have come to pass since I last wrote in this. A distinguished literary gent has been kind enough to pay me a little praise for my efforts at literature. I am in the Senior too, now, and in the middle of writing a play that I cannot write. It is sticking lamentably. One last thing. They have given me a different room, and have put a new carpet into the new room for luck. And this smells rather like a tannery. Consequently I am being slowly poisoned. "Ai vai!"

12 October

Really, Noat is amazing. Last night the President of the Essay Society, who is a master, wrote to ask me to join it. I refused; I am sick of Societies. This evening J. W. P. sends for me, and tells me he has heard about it and that I must join. Compulsion. Think of it – being made to join! Of course I can't go now. I shall join formally and never look at it. It is extraordinary.

Am reading *Crime and Punishment* by Dostoievsky. What a book! I do not understand it yet. It is so weird and so big that it appals me. What an amazing man he was, with his epileptic fits which were much the same as visions really.

20 October

About a week ago I finished *Crime and Punishment*. It is a terrible book, and has had a profound effect. Technically speaking, it is badly put together, but it cuts one open, tragedy after tragedy, like a chariot with knives on the wheels. The whole thing is so ghastly that one resents D. harrowing one so. And then it ends, in two pages. But what a *finale*! Sonia, too, what she suffered. And the scene when she read the Bible.

I have tried to read *The Idiot*, and have finished *Fathers and Sons*, by Turgeniev, but it was a dream only. It is a most dreadful, awful, supremely great book, this Crime and its Punishment. And the death scene, with her in the flaming scarlet hat, and the parasol that was not in the least necessary at that time of day. With the faces crowding through the door, and the laughter behind. What a scene! And the final episode, in Siberia, by the edge of the river that went to the sea where there was freedom, reconciliation, love.

What a force books are! This is like dynamite.

Extract from a letter written by B. G. to Seymour.

Sat., 7 April

"Dear Seymour,

"An awful thing has happened. John is blinded. Mrs Haye, his stepmother, you know, wrote a letter from Barwood which reached me this morning. The doctors say he hasn't a chance of seeing again. She has asked me to write to all his school friends and to you. It is a terrible story. Apparently he was going home after Noat had 'gone down,' on Thursday, that is. The train was somewhere between Stroud and Gloucester, and was just going to enter a cutting. A small boy was sitting on the fence by the line and threw a big stone at the train. John must have been looking through the window at the time, for the broken glass caught him full, cut great furrows in his face, and both his eyes are blind for good. Isn't it dreadful? Mrs Haye says that he suffers terribly. It is a tragedy. Blindness, the most . . ." etc.

Part Two

CHRYSALIS

CHAPTER I

News

Outside it was raining, and through the leaded window panes a grey light came and was lost in the room. The afternoon was passing wearily, and the soft sound of the rain, never faster, never slower, tired. A big bed in one corner of the room, opposite a chest of drawers, and on it a few books and a pot of false flowers. In the grate a weary fire, hissing spitefully when a drop of rain found its way down the chimney. Below the bed a yellow wardrobe over which large grain marks circled aimlessly, on which there was a full-length glass. Beyond, the door, green, as were the thick embrasures of the two windows green, and the carpet, and the curtains.

The walls were a neutral yellow that said nothing, and on them were hung cheap Italian crayon drawings of precocious saints in infancy. The room was called the Saints' Room. Behind the glass of each were hundreds of dead flies, midges, for the room had a strange attraction for these things in summer, when the white ceiling would be black with them by sunset. With winter coming on they would creep away under the glass to pine on attendant angel lips. Perhaps the attraction was rather the hot-water cistern that was under the roof just above, and which gave a hint of passion to the virgin whitewash.

He lay in bed, imagining the room. To the left, on the dressing-table by the bed, would be the looking-glass that would never stay the right level. It would be propped up with a book, so that it gazed blandly up at the ceiling, mimicking the chalky white, and waiting for something else to mimic. On the chair between table and bed was sitting the young trained nurse, breathing stertorously over a book.

There came quick steps climbing stair carpet, two quick steps at the top on the linoleum, and the door opened. Emily Haye came in. She was red, red with forty years' reckless exposure to the sun. Where neck joined body, before the swift V turned the attention to the mud-coloured jumper knitted by herself, there glowed a patch of skin turned by the sun to a deeper red. She was wearing rough tweeds, and she was smelling of soap, because it was near tea-time.

He turns his head on the pillow, the nurse rises, and Mrs Haye walks firmly up the room.

"Well, how are you?"

"All right, thanks."

"I'll sit by him for a bit, nurse, you go and get your tea. It's rainin' like anything outside. I went for a walk, got as far as Wyleman's barn, and there I turned and came back. Stepped in and saw Mrs Green's baby. It's her first, so she's making a fuss of it; beautiful baby, though. Have you been comfortable?"

"Yes, thanks."

"Get any sleep?"

"No."

"Is it hurting you much now?"

"Just about the same."

"It's too wretched for you, this thing comin' right at the beginning of the holidays. I should be very angry, but you seem to be takin' it calmly; you are always like that, you know, John, always hiding things. I was talking with the specialist just as he was going – and he says that you probably will not be able to go back to Noat next term. So you will miss your last term, which is so important they tell me. It means so much to you in after-life, or something. I know Ralph always used to say that it had meant a great deal to him, the responsibility and all that. But I expect you're glad."

36

"Of course. Father may have had some responsibility, but they would never have given any to me, however long I stayed there. I was too incompetent. Can you imagine me enforcing authority?"

"I think that you would be excellent in authority, I do really. But as Mabel Palmer was saying at tea the other day, you never seemed to have any of the ambition of ordinary boys – to be captain of football or cricket, and so on. I did so want to be a boy when I was a girl. I wanted to be good at cricket, and they never let us play in those days."

"You would have made a fine cricketer, Mamma. But I don't think you would have thought much of school life, if you had gone there. You wouldn't have been as wretched as I was, but you would have seen through it, I think. You don't judge people now by their goodness at games, do you?"

"You know you weren't wretched, and – oh, well, we mustn't argue. John, what's it like with that thing in front of your eyes so that you can't see anything? What's it feel like?"

"I don't know, everything's black, that's all."

What was it in the air? Why were they talking in long sentences, importantly?

"I should go mad if I were like that, not to be able to see where one is going. John dear, you are very patient, I shouldn't be nearly as good as you."

"I can quite imagine that. But it won't be for so very long?"

Why had he ended with a question?

"Well, we must be practical. And the specialist was telling me it would be quite a long time before – before you would be up and about again. But doctors always exaggerate, you know. And there's your poor face to get well besides."

"But how long will it be before I shall be able to take this damned head-dress off in daylight? It was all very well when the old fool took it off in the darkened room so that I

37

couldn't see anything, nor he either. His breath did smell nasty, too."

"My dear boy, I never notice people's breath."

" 'May be the sign of a deep-rooted disorder.' 'Even your best friends won't tell you.' 'Halitosis is an insidious enemy,' and so on. And an American firm has got the only thing on God's earth that will cure you. He ought to take it, really."

"John, I do wish you would not swear like that. The servants would be very shocked if they knew, and it is such a bad example to the village boys."

"But, heavens above, they don't hear me swear."

"No, but they hear of it, don't you see."

– Must talk. "Rather an amusing thing has happened. You know Doris, the third housemaid. Well, she is little more than a child, and hasn't got her hair up. When she came, of course I insisted that she should put it up, which upset her terribly. Now, when she takes the afternoon off she puts it into a pigtail again. Silly little thing."

"What's that in your voice? You aren't angry with her, are you? because I think it's rather nice. I like pigtails, don't you? Do you know that bit of Browning, *Porphyrias' Lover*? But when shall I be able to see a pigtail again, that's the point?"

"What's that thing, John, a poem, or what?"

"He makes her lover strangle her with her own hair, done in a pigtail. I don't know what it means, no one knows, only I am quite sure I should like to do it. Think – the soft, silken rope, and the warm, white neck, and . . ."

"Now, don't be silly. I don't understand."

"But when shall I be allowed to take this off? It will be fun seeing again. I suppose he gave some idea of a date?"

"Yes, but he was not very definite, in a way he was rather vague. You see, it is a long business. Eyes are delicate things."

Dread.

"How long? – three months? I only thought it would be one, but it can't be helped."

"Longer than that, I am afraid. Much longer, he said."

"Six months?"

"Dear boy, we must be practical. It may take a – a very long time indeed."

"In fact, I shall be blind for life. Why didn't you tell me at once? No, no, of course I understand."

So he was blind.

She looks out of the window into the grey blur outside. Drops are having small races on the panes. The murmur fills the room with lazy sound. Now and then a drop falls from an eave to a sill, and sometimes a little cascade of drips patter down.

His heart is thumping, and there is a tightness in his throat, that's all. She had not actually said that he was blind. It wasn't he. All the same she hadn't actually said – but he was blind. Blind. Would it always be black? No, it couldn't. Poor Mamma, she must be upset about it all. What could be done? How dreadful if she started a scene while he was lying there in bed, helpless. But of course he wasn't blind. Besides, she hadn't actually said. What had she said? But then she hadn't actually said he wasn't. What was it? He felt hot in bed, lost. He put out a hand, met hers, and drew it away quickly. He must say something. What? (Blind? Yes, blind.) But . . .

"We must be practical, John darling, we must run this together." – Darling? She never used that. What was she saying? ". . . bicycles for two, tandems they're called, aren't they? Work together, let me do half the work like on a tandem bicycle. Your father and I went on a trip on one for our honeymoon, years ago now, when bicycles were the latest thing. I wish he was here now, he was a wonderful man, and he would have helped, and – and he would have known what to do."

"What was he like?" (So he was blind, how funny.)

39

"Dear boy, he was the finest man to hounds in three counties, and the most lovely shot. I remember him killing fifty birds in sixty cartridges with driven grouse at your grandfather's up in Scotland. A beautiful shot. He would have helped."

"It's all right, I guessed it all along, you see. I knew it really when the man was looking at me in what he said was darkness. There was something in his manner. Christ! my eyes hurt, though."

"Dear boy, don't swear like that. No, it can't be your eyes that hurt; if they did it would be a very good thing. It's your face that – that is cut up rather. Not that all hope is gone, of course, there is still a chance, there always is, the specialist said so. Miracles have happened before now. But I do hate your swearing like this."

"I'm sorry."

Why had she died, who could have helped him so much now? All these years he had thought so little about her, and now she was back, and she ought to be sitting by the bed, and she would be helping so much, and there would be nothing to hide, and it would be so much simpler if Mummy were here. Her hands would drive away the pain. It would be so different.

"But I will read to you, all your nice books. And then you will go on writing just the same; you could dictate to me. I shall always be there to help, we'll see it out together."

Heaven forbid. She would never be able to read Dostoievsky, would never be able to understand. Besides, poor dear,·it would bore her so except for the first few weeks when she would feel a martyr, and that was never a feeling to encourage. And how fine it would be to renounce her help in seeing it through, not as if it ever had an end, but how unselfish. Why was there no one else?

"Thank you, darling."

What had he said? He ought never to have said that, it gave the whole show away. Why did one's voice go? But what was there to say? He was blind, finished, on the shelf, that was all. Still, he must carry her through. She must be dreadfully upset about it all. But what was there to say?

She was struggling.

"It's all right, it's not so bad as it looks, it's not as if we were very poor, it could – much worse, much worse."

How wonderful he was, taking it like this, just like Ralph. She would like to say so many things, she longed to, but he did so hate demonstrativeness. She must try to say the right thing, she must not let it run away with her. And she must talk to keep his mind off.

"You are very brave, dear. I know it would have knocked me up completely, Ralph too. I don't know where you take everything from, I can't understand you half the time, you're not a bit like the family, though Mabel told me the other day that you are getting Ralph's profile as you grow older, but I can't see it. You know God gave you your sight and He has taken it away, but He has left us each other, you know, and . . ."

"Yes, yes."

There, she had done it. But it was all true, it must be true. She must not make that mistake again.

It wasn't fair to say that as he was helpless. And what business was it of hers? – he wasn't hers. Why did these things happen? Why did she sit there? It was so hard. And the pain.

"Yes. Mummy, of course."

Mummy, he hadn't used that for so long.

It would not happen again. Her feelings had betrayed her. The great thing was to keep his mind off. One must just go on talking, and it was so hard not to harp on it. A silence would be so terrible. There was always her between them. And it was not right, it was not as if the woman had ever done anything for him, except, of course, to bring him into the world. But it was she who had brought him up. He belonged to her.

41

"I am afraid I shall never be a good mother to you, John. I don't understand anything except out-of-door things, and babies. You were a lovely baby when you were small, and I could do everything for you then, and I loved it. But now you've outgrown me in a way and left me behind. As I was saying to Mabel the other day, I don't understand the young generation, you're too free about everything, though in many ways you yourself are an exception to that, with your secretiveness. I don't know how it is, but young people seem to care less about the country than they did. Now you, John, when you went – go for a walk, you mooch about, as old Pinch would say. And when you come back you don't eat a decent meal, but in that nice phrase, you are all mimmocky with your grub."

She laughed tremulously, then hurried on. He smiled at the old friend, though his mouth seemed afraid.

"I believe it all comes from this cigarette smoking, that's what Ralph used to say, and I think it's true. Nasty as his pipe was, at least it was healthy. You are all either too difficult and unapproachable, or too talkative. That Bendon girl a few days ago at Mrs Pender's told me all her most private and intimate affairs for a whole hour after having met me for the first time. In the old days the girl would have been thought improper. She was the sort of girl your grandfather would have smiled at. He . . ."

"Mamma!" This was better.

"Eh?"

"Nothing."

"He always smiled at something he could not understand, and what he could not understand he could not, and of course there was something wrong in it if he could not. In the old days . . ."

She was off again, and how the old days thrilled her generation, how blind they were not to see the glories of the present and future! Blind. Perhaps in years to come his memories would be only of the time when he had seen the colours and life through his own eyes. But he was becoming sentimental, and surely he had recovered from that phase of his Noat days. What is she saying? (Blind? Yes, blind.) What?

". . . don't understand." – The strain of talking to him of other things!

"But why try? Parents will never understand their children. Have you read Turgeniev's *Fathers and Sons*? There's a wonderful picture there."

He had not been listening. She had not been able to understand the bailiff's policy with the pigs. And here he was on to his books again, as if books mattered in life. But one must always show interest, so that he might feel he had someone who took a kindred interest. One had read all those Russian things in one's teens. One had loved them then, but one saw now what nonsense they had been.

"Yes, I read it years ago, when I married. I don't remember much, but I don't think it was a tremendously interesting book, do you, dear?"

There, they are always like that, "Yes, I read it years ago." Nothing lives for them but the new, they have forgotten everything else, life itself even! She has always read a book, any book you care to mention, and she has always forgotten all about it, save that she has read it. Irritation! She was dead, withered through not caring, and he was alive, how alive he was! Alive ! Alive? And blind, a tomb of darkness, with all the carbuncles of life hidden away! Blind? Yes, blind for ever, always, always blind! No. What is she saying? Nothing, there is silence save for the silken rustling of the rain outside. She must be ill at ease.

"Yes," he says, as one throws a lifebelt at someone drowning.

"Dear, I meant to help, and here I am, swearing away just the same. I'm not much of a mother to you, I'm afraid . . ." Was there no way to help him? When you tried to make him respond to affection he withdrew into himself

43

at once. She would cry if she stayed here much longer. Why did these tragedies come like this? And they were like strangers.

"... don't, of course not. Of course you help, because I can feel that there is someone there, someone standing by who can really help when I want it. That's what you are to me, a real friend."

The weather had beaten all real sympathy out of her. She was so hard, so desperately rugged. There was a great deal to be said against going out in the rain. Hot-house flowers were better than hardy annuals, but then he would never understand the names of flowers now. Mrs Fane was the ideal, so tantalising, so feminine. Mummy would have been like that. And now he would never see a painting, he would just become a vegetable like Mamma, a fine cabbage. And he would have had such a marvellous time with flowers, and with women, who were so close to flowers. But what was this? One must not slobber, sentimentality was intolerable. But how nice to slobber sometimes.

What's that she was saying, a story? Which one? Ah, yes, the new one, about the waste of pig-wash.

There's the rain outside, and the chuckling of the gutter pipes. It will be grey in the room now, or is it dark? Blind, so he didn't know. Light, no more light. And if he were to lift the bandages, surely there was only that between him and light, not a whole lifetime. There is a click.

"Is that the light on?"

"Yes, dear. Well, I must go to tea. Don't let it all worry you too much, dear." She could not bear it any more.

And she was gone. What did she mean by her "and don't let it all worry you too much"? Worry? Worry? He was blind. They did not seem to realise that he was blind, that he would never see again. Nothing but black. Why, it was absurd, stifling. He was blind and they did not mind that he was blind and would never see again. But it was silly to say that you would never see anything again, that was impossible. You could not see black for ever, you would have to see something, or you would go mad. Mad. So he was blind. He had always heard of blind people. But of course it meant absolutely nothing. It was silly.

There were slow steps up stair carpet, three wavering steps on the linoleum, and the door opened. Nanny comes in.

"Master John, I have brought you your tea."

She puts something down that clinks.

"Thanks."

"Did you have a nice sleep?"

"No."

"Would you like a nice cup o' tea, Master John?"

Was everything nice and like her religion, comfortable?

"All right, Nan."

He was being very good. Tea drinking was a vice in some walks of life, and in tea there was tannin, a harmful drug. But he was blind, he could not see. And the pain. So that he was like a blind worm in a fire, squirming, squirming to get out.

"Nice hot tea. You love your tea, don't you, Nan?"

"She likes her cup o' tea, your old Nan does, Master John. I always have been partial to a cup o' tea. All through the time when you was in the nursery it helped me along, for you was a bad boy then. An' before that, when you used to lie 'elpless in my arms with yer little red face. Lor', you would 'oller too if yer milk was so much as a minute late. I remember . . ."

She was remembering. Why were they all remembering? But perhaps it was an occasion to do so. They looked back into a past that lived only in their memories, they did not see the present, the birth of a new life, of a new art, and his life which had changed so suddenly. But he had lived his life, as Nan had lived hers, he must now look back. And it would be so comfortable being sentimental, and talking about memories. For to look back was the only thing left, to look forward was like thinking of nothing. Still, it could not all be over, there must be something in the future, something beyond these black walls! Romantic again. She too, ". . . with yer grasp in yer little hand . . ." she was maudlin. Magdalen, he was to have gone there. Oxford. No. Prehensile, that is all a baby is, and the nurse a ministrant at the knees of Moloch, the supreme sentimentalist. But her feelings were hurt so easily, and her tears were terrible. He must be good.

". . . a lovely babby . . ."

"What is there for tea, Nan?"

"Well, I thought you might like buttered toast and bread and butter, you always was that fond of at nursery teas, and the Easter cake . . ."

"I'll break the rules and have a bit of that first, Nan, please."

She cuts a slice and begins to feed him bit by bit, at intervals putting the teacup into his hands. She loves doing it. For years she has watched him getting more and more independent, and now she is feeding him again. It is nice.

Her hand trembles, she has been garrulous and reminiscent, while she is usually sparing of unnecessary words. She has been told that he is blind, of course that's it. So that will mean more sympathy, if not expressed – which would be intolerable – at any rate only just underneath the surface. But how could you escape it? There were the people who had seen him grow up, and who inevitably had a possessive interest in him. They cared for him through no fault of his own, like dogs, and were sorry for the pain they felt in themselves at his blindness. They were busy dramatising it all to him, while he wanted to be alone, alone to patch up his life. And now he was being theatrical!

"Would you like a sip of tea again, Master John?"

"Thanks, and some buttered toast."

"I do so love feeding ye, Master John, like I used to with the bottle. I remember . . ."

46

There would be red round her eyes, there would be a tell-tale weakness about her lips. He could see her looking at him with the smile he used to notice on parents' faces in Chapel at Noat, while they were saying to themselves, all through the service, that they had been through just what the boy was going through now, though what it was they didn't know. They were saying that they had read the book, years ago. And she was remembering him when he had hardly been alive, she was gloating, gloating that he was weak and helpless again. He would have to have her near him day after day, while she bombarded him with her sickening sentimentality. But what was he doing, eating like this, with this tragedy of darkness upon him? And the pain, the pain.

"No, no, take it away. I don't want any more, I couldn't."

"Oh, Master John, don't take on so."

And the poor old face is falling in, and he hears her beginning to sob. Then she is groping for the chair, to sit, bowed, in it. This was terrible, it bordered on a scene, and he was helpless. He shrank and shrank till he was shrivelled up. The whole creed was strength and not giving way. He gives her his hand, which she takes in her skinny, trembling ones, and tears fall on it, one by one, with little sploshes that he feels rather than hears. Poor Nanny.

But of course she must have been crying in the servants' hall before this, banking, minting on the fact that she had known him longer than anyone else there. The cook and Mamma's maid had been most attentive and sympathetic, the kitchen-maid had wept with her. Only the trained nurse did not listen, she would have sat apart reading, for she knew what youth was, the others had forgotten it. He could see the scene, with Nan babbling on through her tears. That fatuous line of Tennyson's, "Like summer tempests came her tears." But there was coming a serious Tennyson revival.

47

The trained nurse understood youth from the way her hand caressed his bandages, they had not trained it out of her yet, nor had life. But everyone else was like that, everyone except B. G. He wanted B. G., who would understand, who was the only person who would feel what he was feeling, and who would sympathise in the right way.

She struggled to her feet, letting go of his hand.

"You mustn't mind me, Master John, I'm only an old woman."

And she went out slowly. So she had gone. But he was blind, everyone would be sorry for him, everyone would try to help him, and everyone would be at his beck and call; it was very nice, it was comfortable. And he would take full advantage, after all he deserved it in all conscience. He would enjoy life: why not? But he was blind. He would never be able to go out in the morning and recognise the sweep of lawn and garden again, and to wonder that all should be the same. He would never again be able to appreciate the miracle that anything could be so beautiful, never to see a bird again, or a cloud, or a tree, or a horse dragging a cart, or a baby blowing bubbles at his mother! Never to see a flower softly alive in a field, never to see colour again, never to watch colour and line together build up little exquisite temples to beauty. And the time when he had gone down on his knees before a daffodil with Herrick at the back of his mind, how he had grown drunk before it. And then the thought of how finely poetic he must be looking as he knelt before a daffodil in his best flannel trousers. What a cynic he was! That was another of his besetting sins. What a pity, also, to be so self-conscious. The pain.

The misery of hating himself as much as he did. How unlucky he was to have been born like that, so infinitely superior to the common ruck. The herd did not feel all that he did, all his private tortures, and he was unfit to die like this, shut up in the traditional living tomb. A priest ought to have said offices over him as the glass entered his head and caused the white-hot pains there. And now the darkness pressed down on him, and he was not ready. He was not sufficient in himself. He did not know. He had been wandering off on expeditions in a mental morass before, and now all chance of retreat was cut off. He must live on himself, on his own reserves of mental fat, which would be increased a trifle perhaps when Mamma or Nan read to him, as steam rollers go over roads, levelling all sense, razing all imagery to the ground with their stupidity. And when he learned Braille it would be too slow. And it terrifies, the darkness, it chokes. Where is he? Where? What's that? Nothing. No, he is lost. Ah, the wall, and he is still in bed and has hurt his hand in the blow he gave it. The bell should be here to the left – yes, here it is, how smoothly everything goes if you keep your head. His hand tastes salt, he must have skinned it against the wall.

There are steps on stair carpet, four quick steps on the linoleum, and the nurse enters, prettily out of breath.

"Well, and how are we? Did you ring, Mr John? I am so sorry, I was having my tea."

"Oh, nurse, I was frightened. Look, I have skinned my knuckles, haven't I?"

"Silly, whatever did you do that for? That was very naughty of you. Now I shall have to bind it up."

She washes it . . . She has such a pretty voice that he would like to squeeze her hand as she is holding his. And he wanted sympathy. But it would be too terrifying, he had had enough awkward scenes to-day, he did not feel strong enough for another if she were to object. And a nice sight he must be with bandages all over him. Besides, being a professional, she would not be intrigued by bandages as others might. No, he could do nothing.

And she? Well, he wasn't a very interesting case, was he? It was not as if he had left in their sockets, eyes that needed fighting for to save. There was nothing interesting in his condition. How she loved difficult cases. She had only just graduated, so she hadn't had any. And he was quite healthy, he was really healing very quickly, and he hadn't a trace of shock. They had always told her in the profession that she would soon get out of it once she had had one, but her dream was a case of *delirium tremens*; to hear the patient describe the blue mist and the snakes, snakes crawling over everything. But she hadn't had one yet. They fought, there had to be two of you, it kept your hands full. She was sorry for the poor boy, but then he was not really suffering. Suffering made you a great well of pity, and that of course was love.

Her hands felt the bandages and then started work. The pain redoubles, torn face with white-hot bars of pain shooting across it. He was in agonies. He was like a bird in a white-hot cage, the pain pursuing him wherever he turned, and he began to squirm, physically now, in bed. Agony filled his head and his body and everything of him. She was changing the dressing, it would be over soon, and he must not moan, for that was not strong or beautiful. Aah. There, he had done it, and the pain died down again to the old glow. She had finished and he had moaned just a second before everything had been over. All for nothing, and it did not seem much now. She was despising him for moaning, he could sense it. And the athlete would have riddled his lips with his strong teeth before he uttered a sound, and then only to ask for a cigarette. Poor woman. And he was blind, was he?

So that he would grow on into a lonely old age. He would know his way round the house, and there would be his favourite walk in the garden. As all blind men he would do everything by touch, and he would have tremendous powers of hearing. He would play music divinely, on the gramophone. And the tears would course from behind his sightless eyeballs – but had he any? He had never thought of that. He felt with his hand, but the bandages were too tight. He remembered that men with amputated legs could still waggle the toes which by that time were in the dustbin. He squinted, and was sure that his eyes were there.

"Nurse, have I any eyes?"

"How do you mean? No, I am afraid they were both taken out, they had to be."

It had been a dull operation, and they were now in spirits on the mantelpiece of her room at home in the hospital. When she got back she was going to put them just where she could see them first thing every morning, with the toes and the kidney. She had had an awful trouble to get the eyes.

Oh, so his eyes were gone. Now that was irritating, a personal loss. Dore had been furious because his appendix had been removed the term before last, he said it was a blemish on his personal beauty, but eyes were much more personal. Why hadn't they taken the eyes of one of the "muddied oafs"? While he, he was blind. How had it happened? He had never asked; must have been some accident or something. He would ask.

"Nurse, how did it happen?"

"Do you think you can bear to talk about it?"

"Why not?"

"Well, a small boy threw a stone at the train, and it broke your window as you were looking out. It was very careless of him. But what I can't understand is your being unconscious immediately like that, and not remembering. But doctor said you could be told, and . . ."

A small boy. Damn him.

"And what happened to the small boy?"

"He was whipped by the police yesterday. Won't you try and get some sleep now?" and her hands smooth the pillow disinterestedly and tuck him up. Before, when he had remembered it, this had been deliciously thrilling. So a small boy in a fit of abstraction, or of boredom, had blinded him, a small boy who could not appreciate what he had done, at least only for so long as his bottom hurt him. Why, if he had the child, he would choke him. One's fingers would go in and in till they would be enveloped by pink, warm flesh. The little thing would struggle for a while, and then it would be over, you know, just a tiny momentary discomfort for an eternity of pleasure, for were not his godparents shouldering his sins for him? It would be a kindness to the little chap, and one would feel so much better for it afterwards. He would be apprehended for murder, and he would love it. He would make the warder read the papers to him every morning, he would be sure to have headlines: BLIND MAN MURDERS CHILD – no, TORTURES CHILD TO DEATH. And underneath that, if he was lucky, WOMAN JUROR VOMITS, something really sensational. Mr Justice Punch, as in all trials of life and death, would be amazingly witty, and he would be too. He would make remarks that would earn him some famous title, such as THE AUDACIOUS SLAUGHTERER. All the children in England would wilt at his name. In the trial all his old brilliancy would be there. Talking. No more of those conversations that had been so tremendously important. No more snubs, no more bitternesses, for the rest of his life he would be surrounded by dear, good, dull people who would be kind and long-suffering and good, and who would not really be alive at all. How dull being good for ever, always being grateful and appreciative for fear of hurting their feelings. And never to see again, how important transparency was. His head was beginning to hurt again. Nothing but women all his life. Better to have died. Why didn't the pain go away?

What was the time?

Her, Him, Them

"Good morning, mum."

"Grmn', J'net."

And Janet, after putting the can of hot water in the basin behind the screen, went to the red curtains and pulled them back. The sunlight leapt, catching fire on her fuzzy hair, and the morning came freely in by the open windows. Mrs Haye, in the right half of the double-bed, had such a lost look in the eyes which were usually so imperious that Janet shook her head sadly.

She had had a bad night, the first since Portgammon over the fireplace there had fallen with her jumpin' timber and had broken his back. She would get up immediately, it was no use stickin' here in this ghastly bed. Pity she did not take her bath in the morning, a bath now would do her good. But there was more need for it in the evening.

"Janet, I will get up and dress now."

"Now'm?"

"Yes, now."

Later: "Will you have the brown tweed or the green'm?"

"The heather mixture. Janet, these stockings each have a hole in the heel. I wish you would not put me out stockings that are unfit to wear."

She was in one of her tempers to-day, and no wonder. But as cook had said at supper last night, "No one to give notice till a year 'as passed by."

She was washing behind the screen, splashing and blowing. Then her teeth were being attacked. Work and forget, work and forget, till some plan emerged. She would send for Mabel Palmer and they would talk it out.

She almost fell asleep while Janet was doing her hair.

Diving upwards through the heather-mixture skirt, she said, "Tell William to ring up Mrs Palmer Norbury 27, you know, to ask her if she will come to tea to-day."

"Yes'm."

She struggled into the brown jumper and before the look-ing-glass put in the fox-head pin. There was old Pinch in the herbaceous border doing nothing already. She had never seen him about so early, it was really extraordinary. She looked a long time at Ralph in his photograph, but he was absolutely the same. His smile said nothing, gave her no advice, but only waited to be told what to do, just as he had been obeying the photographer then. He would have had more in common with the boy perhaps, would have been able to talk to him of pig-sticking out in India in the old 10th days. She could do nothing to distract him. But then he didn't hunt, he didn't shoot, he only fished and that sitting down, and he couldn't fish now. Perhaps it was just as well he had given up huntin', it would have been terrible had that been taken away from her suddenly.

How heavy her skirt felt, and she was stiff. She felt old to-day, really old: this terrible affair coming suddenly like this, just when the Nursing Association was beginning to go a little better, too. And she could do nothing for the poor boy, nothing. But something must be done, there must be some way out. Of course, he would never see again, it was terrible, she had seen that the first time the doctors saw her at the hospital, where that appalling woman was head nurse. She had not had a ward all through the war for nothing, she had seen at once. Some occupation must be found for him, it was the future one had to think about, and Mabel Palmer might know of something. Or his friends might – but then he hadn't any, or at any rate she had never seen them. There it was, first Ralph falling down dead of

54

his heart on the stairs, and now fifteen years after her boy was blinded, worse than being dead. What could one say to him? What could one do?

She went downstairs. In the Oak Hall she found the dog, who rose slowly to greet her, looking awkwardly in her direction.

"You, Ruffles? Why have they let you out so early? Poor blind old thing. Oh, so old."

She scratched his neck gently. Would it be better to have him destroyed? He was so old, he could hardly see any more, and it hurt him to bark. What enjoyment could he get out of life, lying there by the fire, asleep all day and hardly eating at all? Yet he had been such a good servant, for ten years he had barked faithfully at friends. And the only time he had not barked was when the burglars had come that once, when they had eaten the Christmas cake, and had left the silver. But it would be kinder to put him out of the way. One must be practical. But he was blind!

William came in by the dining-room door carrying one of the silver inkstands as if it had been a chalice. His episcopal face was set in the same grave lines, his black tail-coat clung reverently to a body as if wasted by fasting, his eyes, faithfully sad, had the same expression of respectful aloofness. William, at least, never changed. She remembered so well old Lady Randolph, who had known him fifty years ago when he was at Greenham, saying, "I see no change in William." But of course her eyesight had not been very grand, nevertheless William had shown distant pleasure when told. Still he was too aged, he could not do his share of the work, it must all fall on Robert; the boy was so lazy, though, that it would be good for him to do a little extra. But what could one do? He had served her for years, he had been a most conscientious servant, and it was only the night when the burglars did come that he had been asleep. However, they had only eaten the Christmas cake, they had left the silver.

"William, I should like breakfast as soon as possible."

"Very well, madam."

And he was gone. Yes, it was convenient to have him about. He was quiet, he never exceeded himself, and he understood.

Outside, on the little patch of lawn up to the drive, they were mowing already with the horse-mower. They had made a very early start. The same George, the same Henry leading the pony which had carried John across the open country behind the hounds before he had given up, and which was still the same. It was only John who had changed.

"George," she cried, "George."

The pony halted by himself, the men listened.

"George, see that no stones get in the blades, it ruins them. Henry, you must pick them up and throw them back on to the drive."

Both: "Yas'm."

And they went on mowing.

Of course they were going to keep her waiting for her breakfast now. But no, William came in and gravely announced it.

As she went in she looked gratefully at him, he was a symbol. He had come to them directly after the honeymoon, prematurely white and sad. Ralph used to say that he was a marvellous valet. Thirty years ago. Then they had gone to India with the 10th. Ten years after they had come back, and had found William again. It was extraordinary, that, and Ralph had said then that he tasted comfort for the first time in ten years. At the funeral William had sent his own wreath, on it written in his copy-book handwriting, "To his master respectfully from his valet." It had not been tactful, she had had to thank him. He had exceeded himself. His only lapse.

Nothing seemed worth while. Yesterday had tired her out utterly. First the doctors destroying her last bit of hope, and then her breaking it to him, which had been so terrible.

She had gone up again after tea, and it had been frightful, his face underneath the bandages had been tortured, his mouth in a half-sneer. She had been frightened of him. And finally, as nicely as he could, he had asked her to leave him for the evening. The nurse had met her at the door and had whispered, "He is in rather a state," as if she had not known that. The woman was a fool.

This coffee was undrinkable. The cook had probably been gigglin' again with Herbert. That affair! You could not drink it, absolutely undrinkable. She would make a row. But was it worth while? She felt so tired to-day. But the house must go on just as usual, there must be no giving way. She rang the bell. They must find some occupation for the boy, he could not be left there rankling. Making fancy baskets, or pen-wipers, all those things blinded soldiers did, something to do. William coughed.

"William, this coffee is undrinkable. Will you tell the cook to find some occupation for . . . to find some . . . The roaster must be out of order. No, don't take my cup away. I will drink it for this once."

Had he seen? At any rate he would not tell. She had not been able to give a simple order, it was terrible, without giving herself away. She must make inquiries about Braille books, and find someone to teach it to him. A knock.

"Come in."

It was the nurse.

"Good morning, Mrs Haye. I came down because I wish you would come up to speak to John. He has refused to eat his breakfast, and there was a nice bit of bacon this morning. I am afraid he is taking it rather badly, he did not sleep much last night. But if you would come up and get him quieter."

What right had she to call him John? She must be changed. Oh, the misery of it, and the tortures he must be going through. She could do nothing, if she spoke to him she would only say the wrong thing.

57

She rose from the table and looked at the coffee-pot.

"I can do nothing with him, nurse. I think it would be better to leave him to himself, he always prefers that. He will be quieter this evening."

"Very good, Mrs Haye; I dressed his wounds this morning, they are getting on nicely."

His wounds. The scars. And he would wear black spectacles. He had been so handsome. It would be better not to go up this morning, but let him quieten down.

She sat down and looked out of the windows in the bay. The big lawn was before her, they would begin to mow it soon. Dotted over it were blackbirds and thrushes looking for worms, and in the longer grass at the bottom she could see the cock pheasant being very cautious. They were pretty things to look at, but he and his two wives did eat the bulbs so. She would have to send for Brown to come down and kill them. And what good was it keeping up the shootin', now that all hope had gone of his ever holdin' a gun? But nothing must change. The lower border was really looking very fine, the daffodils were doing splendidly. It was just the same, the garden, and how well it looked now. He hadn't eaten his breakfast. No. Of course, once in a while a tree fell down and made a gap that would look awkward for a bit, but there were others growing and you became used to it. There went a pigeon, fine birds but a pest, they did more harm to the land than the rooks. She ought never to have made that birthday promise to John, that the garden should be a sanctuary for them; but going out to watch them had made him very happy in the old days, and now? What would he do now?

She got up heavily and left the dining-room. Going through the house she came to the sitting-room, which looked out on to the small rose garden surrounded by a high wall. It ought to look well this year, not that he would see it, though. She had a lot of things to do this morning, she would not let the thing come up and crush her. His was

the sort of nature which needed to be left alone, so it was
no use going up to see him. Plans must be made for when
his new life would begin, and some idea might emerge out
of her work. Being blind he could do work for the other
blind, and so not feel solitary, but get the feeling of a regiment. Meanwhile there was the Nursing Association. She
must write to his friends, too, they ought to know that he
was blind. Would they really care? But of course anyone
who knew John must care. Then their letters would come
in return, shy and halting, with a whole flood of consolation
from the neighbours, half of whom did not care in the least.
She would have to answer them; but no, she couldn't. Then
they would say that the blow had aged her, she had said
that so often herself. Their letters would be full of their own
little griefs, a child who had a cold, a husband worried by
his Indian liver, one who had been cut publicly by Mrs
So-and-So – but this wasn't fair. They would write rather
of someone of theirs who had died recently or years and
years ago, of the memory of their grief then, of what had
helped them then, of prayer, of a wonderful sleeping
draught. Not sleeping, that was what was so hard. And she
would answer suitably, for of course by now one knew
what to say, but it was hateful, people laying little private
bits of themselves bare, and she being expected to do like-
wise. She could say everything to Mabel, but not to them.
Still, it would be all over some day. Life would not be the
same, it would go on differently, and yet really be just the
same. But did that help? Could she say to the boy, "You
will get used to it in time"? It was ridiculous. Could she
preach religion at him when she was not quite sure herself?
Something must be done.

She took up the Nursing accounts. Five pounds in sub-
scriptions, it was not bad. That Mrs Binder. She would
have to write to her, it was ridiculous not to subscribe. She
was the sort of woman to put spider webs on a cut. But
they did not give their babies cider to drink any more as

a substitute for mother's milk, she had stopped that. Yet perhaps Mrs Moon did, she would do anything, and her house was so filthy. The annual inspection had gone off so well, too, the Moon child had been the only one to have nits in her hair. What could one do? The house was filthy, the husband earned very low wages, you could not turn them out for being insanitary, they would have nowhere to go. And the house was losing value every day. John must learn to care about these things.

And her affairs were none too bright. It was as much as one could do to keep the house and the garden going, what with the income tax and the super-tax and everything. The car would have to go, and with it Evans. Harry could drive her about in the dog-cart, it would be like the old days again except when one of them passed her. It was terrible to see the country changing, the big houses being sold, everyone tightening the belt, with the frightful war to pay for. Now that he was blind there was no hope of his ever making any money. And the charities had not stopped. What would happen to John? Even if he hadn't gone blind it would have been difficult enough. There were more charities now, if anything; they came by every post. Her letters, she had forgotten. She rang the bell. That Mrs Walters had written for a subscription to a garden fête in aid of the local hospital. Of course she stole half the money you sent, but a little of it was fairly certain to be used by the hospital. The woman never kept accounts for those things, which was wicked. Then, again, Mrs Andrew and her Parish Nurse, the effrontery of it when she did not subscribe to the Barwood one. What a fight it was. Were there any blind boys in Norbury of his own age, nice boys whom he could make friends with? They could not afford to go to London where he might find some. They could, of course, if they sold Barwood. Sell Barwood! – No, and he would appreciate still having it when he grew older. To be blind in one of those poky little suburban villas, with a wireless set, and with

aeroplanes going overhead, and motor bikes and gramo-
phones. No.

William came in.

What had she rung for? Blank.

"It is all right, William, I have found it now."

It was terrible, she could not even remember when she
rang.

No, everything must go on just the same, the garden
would be still the best in twelve miles, even if all the world
went blind. They must find a companion for the boy, Mabel
would be able to help there. Someone who would spend
his time with him, her time, that would be better. It was
so terrible, he would never marry now, she would have no
grandchildren. The place would be sold, the name would
die, there was no one. Ralph had been the last. "Granny."
He would not meet any nice girls now, he could never
marry. A girl would not want to marry a blind man. All
her dreams were gone, of his marrying, of her going up to
live in the Dower House – that was why the Evanses had
it on a short lease. She would have made friends with his
wife and would have shown her how to run everything.
His wife would have made changes in the house, of course,
and it would have been sad seeing the place different; but
then the grandchildren, and he would have made such a
good father. Why was it taken away quite suddenly like
this? But then they might still find some girl who had had
a story, or who was unhappy at home, who would be glad,
who would not be quite – but who would do. He must
marry. All the bachelors one had known had been so
womanish, old grandfathers without children. John Goe.
She could not fill his life, there would have to be a wife.
Mabel might know of someone. Perhaps they would not
be happy, but they would be married. And she ought to be
happy here, it was a wonderful place, so beautiful with the
garden and the house. It had been her real life, this place;
before she had married she had not counted, something had

just been training her for this. And she had improved it, with the rock garden and the flowers. Mary Haye had not known one flower from another. And she had got the village straight, there had been no illegitimate children for two years, and they were all married. It would be a blow going, a bit of her cut off, but the Dower House was only a mile off, and right in the middle of the village. And now perhaps she would be able to live here till she died if he did not marry. But he must, for his happiness, if there was to be someone to look after him when she died. And she would have grandchildren after all, it might turn out all right, one never knew in this world; there had been Berty Askew. If everything failed he could have a housekeeper. Yes, it was immoral, but he must have love, and someone to look after him. After Grandmamma died the Grandparent had had one at Tarnarvaran. Argyll and the heather . . . Really, now that this trouble was upon her, Edward might write. But it was for him to act first.

She must order dinner. There was comfort in choosing his food, it was something to do for him. Going out she straightened a picture that was a little crooked. As she opened the door the sunlight invaded the passage beyond, and made a square of yellow on the parquet floor.

In front of the swing door into the kitchen she halted. Honestly, one did not like to enter the kitchen now for fear of findin' Mrs Lane gigglin' with Herbert. That affair. Well, if they brought things to a head and married, they would have to leave. She could not bear a married couple among the servants, they quarrelled so.

Inside it was very clean, the deal tables were like butter, the grey-tiled floor, worn in places, shone almost. Along one wall was hung a museum of cooking utensils, every size of saucepan known to science, and sinister shapes. Mrs Lane was waiting. Where was her smile? Oh, of course it was. How nice they all were. Mrs Lane began talking at once.

"I am sorry to say'm that Muriel has had some kittens

in the night. We none of us suspected'm. In the potato box'm."

What, again!

"Tell Harry to drown 'em immediately."

One must be practical.

"If I could find a home for them'm?"

"Very well, Mrs Lane, only I cannot have them here. What with the stable cat and the laundry cat there are too many of 'em about. What is there this morning?"

"Very good'm. I've got a bit of cod for upstairs" – it was no use mentioning no name – "an' would you like one of the rabbits Brown brought in yesterday, and the pigeon pie'm, with cherry tart for upstairs?"

"That will do nicely."

"An' for dinner I . . ." etc.

As she was going out into the kitchen yard so as to gain the stables, Mrs Lane ran after her to stop her. She spoke low and fast.

"Madam, the nurse asked me this morning that she could 'ave 'er meals seprit. Didn't like to take them in the servants' 'all'm."

"If she wants to eat alone, Mrs Lane, we had better humour her. Have them sent up to her room."

"Very good'm."

An' who was to take 'em up to 'er, stuck-up thing?

There, now there was going to be trouble about the nurse. Cook had been angry, although she had tried not to show it. Really they might leave her alone and not bother her with their little quarrels. Somebody would be giving notice in a week. Still, Mrs Lane would not go while Herbert was here.

"Harry, Harry!"

A sound of hissing came suddenly through an open window on the other side of the little yard. A head wobbled anxiously behind a steamy window further down. A hoof clanked.

63

There was the stable cat. "Shoo!"

"Harry!"

"Yess'm."

She inspected the horses and went out.

No, she would not go to the laundry this morning. The damp heat would be rather exhausting. Curry had been riding a nice bay last season which had looked up to her weight. She was getting rather tired of Jolly. She stopped, that had reminded her.

"Harry, you can take them both out to exercise to-morrow, I shall not go out, of course."

"Very good'm."

He would never ride now, all her hopes of getting him back to the love of it were broken, and he could not even go on a lead, for that was so dangerous. What would he do?

She went through the door in the wall into the kitchen garden. She called:

"Weston, Weston!"

There was Herbert pickin' lettuces just for the chance of going to Mrs Lane in the kitchen with them. He raised his bent body and touched his cap. She nodded.

Again she cried:

"Weston!"

A cry came from the other the end, from the middle of the artichokes, the tops of which you could hardly see – it was a big kitchen garden. Weston appeared walking quickly. He took his cap off.

"How are the peaches getting on?"

Peaches were good for convalescents.

"Very nicely'm. Going to be a good crop, and the apples too. Was among the artichokes'm. Fine crop this year. Never seen 'em so high."

"What beautiful cabbages, Weston."

He would eat them, as he could not see flowers.

"Yes'm. Going to be a good crop."

"Yes; well, good morning, Weston."

"Good morning'm."

Into the garden. Pinch was still at the same spot on the border as he had been when she had looked out of her bedroom window. He was too old, but he was a faithful servant.

Yes, his wife was going on as well as was to be hoped. Yes, it was bad weather for the farmers.

Pinch was the same, so why had *he* changed? What was the matter with Pinch's wife? Just age perhaps, any way they would be the next for the almshouses. When Mrs Biggs died they could go in, and that should not be long now. This would leave vacant their cottage on Ploughman's Lane, which that nice man from Huntly could have. How nice the trees were with their fresh green; whatever happened the seasons went round. If this warm weather went on he could get out to be on the lawn, but then you could never tell with the English spring. She would have to go in to write those letters, while it was so lovely out here. There was the moorhen starting her nest in the same place in the moat. Mrs Trench's baby would be due about now, her sixth, while that Jim Pender, earning excellent wages, only had his one girl, and she was five years old. It was ridiculous, she would have to speak to him about it, a great strong fellow like him with such a pretty wife. She must have some jelly and things sent up to Mrs Trench. He must take an interest in the village now that he had nothing to do. He could start a club for the men and teach them something, he would do it very well, talking about art or books, or one of those things he was so interested in. That would do something to occupy his time. There was a daffodil out already, it had planted itself there, it looked so pretty against the bole of the tree. How good a garden was for one! She felt quieter after the ghastly night she had had. The only way out of trouble like this was to work for others till you forgot, when a plan would emerge quite suddenly, that was what life taught one, and Mabel was the same.

Annie was weeding the gravel of the Yew Walk. In summer she weeded, in winter she swept leaves, and she picked up dead branches all the year round.

"Good morning, Annie."

"Good morning'm."

She was not quite all there, poor thing, but there was nothing to be done for her, she would always be like that.

The attendances at church were disgraceful again now, just as bad as when the Shame had had it. That had been the only time the village had been right and she wrong. No one had been able to persuade her till she had seen for herself. It was all part of this modern spirit, she had seen terrible dangers there for him, but now, poor boy, that he was blind she could at least keep him to herself away from those things that led nowhere. She ought to go back now to write those dreadful letters, but it was so lovely out here, with the sunlight. And it didn't look as if it would last, there were clouds about. She had been right to put on thick clothes. How pretty the little stone Cupid was, king of his little garden of wallflowers walled in by yews, it would be a blaze of colour. Now that the flagstones were down you could see what a difference it made.

She opened the door into Ralph's old study. It would be his now, as she had always meant it to be. It got all the sun in the morning, and there were no awkward corners. He would have a hard time at first in getting about, but she would lead him and teach him where the furniture was and all that, it was one of the things she could do for him.

In the Oak Hall there was a note for her. The parson's wife again. Oh, this time she wanted fifty cups and saucers for the Mother's Union tea. Well, she could have them. What, again? No, no, not another. Yes, in the P. S., "I am going to have another darling baby." That was too much. Would they never stop? And they could not afford it with the covey they had already. All it meant was that Mrs Crayshaw would not be able to do any visiting in the village for quite two months. Now there was another letter to write, of congratulation this time, and it was going to be hard to word. What did they call it, a quiver full? To-morrow and there would be another letter from her, she would have heard about him by then, it would be full of earnest stuff. And she did not want sympathy, she wanted practical advice.

It was all so difficult. She had betrayed him this morning, she had not thought nearly enough about it all. She was beginning not to care already. This morning she had frit-tered away, excusing herself by saying that Mabel would think of something, while everyone knew that it was always she who talked while Mabel listened. Still, it was necessary to talk. But last night had been so dreadful, when she had lain in bed turning the thing over and over in her mind, and she had prayed too. She had thought of many ways to occupy his time, but they had all gone out of her head now. Those red curtains were getting faded, but Skeam's man had been insolent when last he came. That was what we were comin' to, a decorator's tout giving himself airs. Before all this she had meant to put John into a decorator's business, he was so artistic that he would have done wonders, perhaps even made a little money. But there, it was no use thinkin' of might-have-beens. He must marry, it was the only thing he could do. He must be a man, and not be left unfinished. They would have the marriage in the church, and a dinner for the tenants in the Great Hall. But he was so young. And she would spend the evenin' of her days in the Dower House.

She passed through the Great Hall. She buried her head violently into a pot of dead roses. In her room Ruffles was sleeping fitfully in his basket. She picked up a paper, glanced at the headlines, then put it aside. She sat in her armchair and looked vacantly at Greylock over the fireplace. Along the mantel-board were ranged a few cards to charities, to funerals, and to weddings. She picked up the paper again and looked through the Society column, and then the deaths and marriages, and then threw it on to the floor. She blew her nose and put the handkerchief away in the pocket of her skirt. She rubbed her face slowly in her hands, when she stopped it was redder still. Then she sat for some time looking at nothing at all, thinking of nothing at all. The specks kept on rising in the sunlight.

She got up. She rang the bell. She went to the writing-table and sat down. She opened the inkstand hoof, Choir-boy's hoof, and she looked at her pens. She dipped one into the ink, and she drew a bit of paper towards her. Then she looked out of the window on to the rose garden for some time.

William came in.

"William, Mrs Crayshaw has written to say that she will want fifty cups and saucers . . . No, on second thoughts . . . It is all right, William, I will go and tell cook myself. And – oh, William, the letters, please."

"Yes, madam."

William held the door open for her. Mrs Lane might not like it from the butler. She would go up to see him after this. But you could not be too careful with servants nowadays, and . . .

★　★　★

How did one pass the time when one was blind? Six days had gone by since she had told him, days filled with the echo of people round occupying themselves on his account. Mamma had had three long conferences with Mrs Palmer, conferences which had reached him through vague refer-ences as to what he was going to do, with not a word as to what he was going to do now. Nan was struggling with an emotion already waning. Her long silences, in which she sent out waves of sentimentality, told that she was trying to freeze what was left into permanency. The nurse helped him grudgingly back to health, the new life was forming, and it was even more boring than the former. They read to him in turn for hours on end, Mamma talked of finding a professional reader. It was now so ordinary to be blind.

He was in the long chair, under the cedar on the lawn. He felt the sky low and his bandages tight. The air nosed furtively through the branches and made the leaves whisper while it tickled his face. Pigeons were cooing, catching each other up, repeating, answering, as if all the world depended on their little loves. It was the sound he liked best about the garden; he yawned and began to doze.

He was alone for the moment. Nan had left him to take a cup of tea. The nurse was taking the daily walk that was necessary to her trade union health, and Mrs Haye had gone up to the village to console Mrs Trench, whose week-old baby was dying. Herbert, leaning on the sill of the kitchen window, was making noises at Mrs Lane while she toyed with a chopper, just out of his reach. Weston was lost in wonder, love and praise before the artichokes, he had a camera in his pocket and had taken a record of their splendour. Twenty years on and he would be showing it to his grandchildren, to prove how things did grow in the old days. Twenty years ago Pinch had seen better. Harry was hissing over a sporting paper; Doris in an attic was letting down her hair, she was about to plait the two soft pigtails. Jenny, the laundry cat, was very near the sparrow now, by the bramble in the left-hand corner of the drying ground.

He roused himself – if he went to sleep it would only mean that he would lie awake all night. He fingered the letter that Nan had read to him from J. W. P., full of regret that he was not coming back next term, saying that he would get his leaving-book from the Headmaster for him. No more going back now, which was one good thing, and no more irritations with J. W. P. He had done a great deal

69

of work, though, that last year; he had really worked quite hard at writing, and he would go on now, there was time when one was blind. J. W. P. had disapproved, of course, and had said that no one should write before he was twenty-one, but about that time he had come under the influence of the small master with spectacles, whose theory was that no boy should have any ideas before he had left school. Perhaps they were right, it was certainly easier to give one-self up to a physical existence. Healthy sanity. And here was weakness, in saying that they ever could be right. But he was in such an appalling desolation that anything might be right. Why had he taken that train?

He felt himself sinking into a pit of darkness. At the top of the pit were figures, like dolls and like his friends, striking attitudes at a sun they had made for themselves, till sinking he lost sight of them, to find himself in the presence of other dolls in the light of a sun that others had made for them. Then it did not work, and he was back in the darkness, on the lawn again. Nothing seemed real.

He said "tree" out loud and it was a word. He saw branches with vague substance blocked round them, he saw lawn, all green, and he built up a picture of lawn and tree, but there were gaps, and his brain reeled from the effort of filling them.

He felt desperately at the deck-chair in which he was sitting. He felt the rough edges of the wood, which would be a buff colour, and he ran a splinter into his finger. He put his hand on the canvas, he knew that it was canvas, dirty white with two red stripes at each side. It felt rough and warm where his body had touched it. He felt for the red, it should have blared like a bugle. It did not; that would come later, perhaps.

He felt the grass, but it was not the same as the grass he had seen.

He lay back, his head hurting him. How much longer would he be here? The letter crinkled in his hands, reminding him of its presence. He ran his fingers over the pages, but he could feel no trace of ink. He came upon the embossed address. It might have been anything. A fly buzzed suddenly. Even a fly could see.

He was shut out, into himself, in the cold.

So much of life had been made up of seeing things. The country he had always looked to for something. He had seen so much in line, so much in colour, so much in everything he had seen. And he had noticed more than anyone else, of course he had.

But when he had seen, how much it had meant. Everything was abstract now, personality had gone. Flashes came back of things seen and remembered, but they were not clear-cut. Little bits in a wood, a pool in a hedge with red flowers everywhere, a red-coated man in the distance on a white horse galloping, the sea with violet patches over grey where the seaweed stained it, silver where the sun rays met it. A gull coming up from beneath a cliff. There was a certain comfort in remembering.

This would have been a good fishing day. There was no sun, yet enough heat to draw the chub up to the surface. The boat would glide silently on the stream, the withies would droop quietly to dabble in the water. Where the two met the chub lay, waiting for something to eat. And he would prepare his rod and he would throw the bright speckled fly to alight gently on the water, and to swim on the current past mysterious doors in the bathing green. The boat floated gently too, a bird sang and then was silent, and he would watch the jaunty fly, watch for the white, greedy mouth that would come up, for the swirl when he would flick lightly, and the fight, with another panting, gleaming fish to be mired in struggles on the muddy floor of the boat.

He would go down the river, catching fish. The day would draw away as if sucked down in the east, where a little rose made as if to play with pearl and grey and blue.

There were chub he had missed, four or five he would have caught, and more further on. A kingfisher might shoot out to dart down the river, a guilty thing in colours. More rarely a grey heron would raise himself painfully to flap awkwardly away. He would go on, casting his fly, placing it here or there, watching it always, and now and then, with little touches, steering it from floating leaves. And it would become more difficult to see, and the only sound would be the plops the fish made as they sent out rings in eating flies on the water. One last chub in the boat and he would turn to row back through the haze that was rising from the river. The water chattered at the prow, he would notice suddenly that the crows were no longer cawing in the trees on the hill, but had gone to sleep. He would yawn and begin to think of dinner. It was a long way back.

He would come to the ferry, where the boats were tied up, where they huddled darkly together. There would be the rattle of the chain, and the feeling that something else was finished. Voices would come from behind the lighted blinds of the inn; a dog would bark, a laugh perhaps, while the other bank was thick with shadows. He would carry the oars and rowlocks to put them as always in the shed, and he would climb the gate, the rod tiresome, the creel heavy. A quick walk home across the fields, for there was nothing to see in the dark. An owl perhaps and a bat or two.

Or again, the river in the heat of an afternoon, stalking from the bank the chub that lay by the withies, and being careful with his shadow. He would wade slowly through long grass with here and there a flower at random, or more often a bed of nettles. He would peer through the leaves that drooped in green plumes to where a chub cruised phantom-like in the cloudy onyx of the water. The sun made other smaller suns that would pierce his eyes and dazzling dance there. Bending low he would draw out as much line as he could. Stooping he would pitch his fly cunningly. The line might fall over the fin, and the fish would be gone.

The chub were hard to catch from the bank, and often it was so hot that the only thing to do was to lie in the shade. There was an alder tree under which lived a rat. He would watch for it sometimes: if one kept still it would come out to play, or to teach a baby what to eat, or to wash in the water. The cattle, bored, might bestir themselves to come and look at him, blowing curiously. The flies would always be tiresome. The water slipped by.

Why was it all over? But it wasn't, he would cultivate his sense of hearing, he would listen to the water, and feel the alder, and the wind, and the flowers. Besides, there had only been about ten fishing days every summer, what with the prevailing wind, which was against the current, raising waves, and the rain in the hills which made mud of the water. There would be no more railing against the bad weather now, which had been half the joy of fishing.

Sometimes, when he was rowing back in the dark after fishing over the sunset below, he had stopped by a withy that he could hardly see, to cast a white fly blindly into the pool of darkness beneath. He would strike by the ripple of light, he had caught two or three fish that way, and it was so mysterious in the twilight. Colours had been wonderful. But these were words only.

What sense of beauty had others? Mamma never said any more than that a thing was pretty or jolly, and yet she loved this garden. She spent hours in weeding and in cutting off the heads of dead roses, and there were long talks with Weston when long names would come out of their mouths – why had some flowers nothing but an ugly Latin name? But you could not say that she had no sense of beauty.

Harry looked upon the country from the hunting standpoint, whether there were many stiff fences and fox coverts. The Arts of Use. And there was Herbert, during the war, at Salonica. The only thing of interest he had remembered afterwards was that a certain flower, that they had here and that was incessantly nursed by Weston in the hot-house, grew wild and in profusion on the hills above the port. Egbert, the underkeeper, at Salonica also, had seen a colossal covey of partridges. That was all they remembered.

In the country one lost all sense of proportion. Mamma used to become hysterical over some ridiculously small matter. Last Christmas it had been ludicrous, she had been so angry, and it had led to one of her outbursts about his not caring for the life here, he, who was to carry on the house and the traditions, and so on. It had been about the Church Parochial Council. She had asked that at matins on Christmas Day there might be music. Crayshaw had answered that there would be music at Holy Communion which took place before, but that as no one ever came to matins on Christmas Day – (And whose fault was that, my dear?) – it was not worth while having music again. There had been a violent discussion, one would have given anything to be there, during which Mamma had said that if she was a child her Christmas would have been ruined with no music on Christmas Day. Crayshaw had replied that the children could come at six in the evening when everyone else came, and when there was music. Mamma had said that it was the morning that mattered. Crayshaw had parried by saying that the children could come to Holy Communion. Mamma had not liked that, "it was bothering children's heads with mysticism." Finally they had voted, and Mamma had been defeated because she had closed the public pathway at the bottom of the garden, a path which no one had used for nine years, and the gates were ugly and in the way. It had spoilt the drive, that wretched path. "The first time, John, that the village has not followed my lead. It is so discouraging." Oh, it had been tragic.

Behind the house a hen was taken with asthma over her newly-laid.

A bee droned by to the accompaniment of flies. He glided down the hill of consciousness to the bottom, where he was aware only of wings buzzing, and of the sun, that poured down a beam to warm him, and of a wind that curled round. Only one pigeon cooed now, and he was tireless, emptying his sentiment into a void of unresponding laziness. He was singing everyone to sleep. How dreadful if a cuckoo were to come. The sky would have cleared, it would be a white-blue. It was hot.

A woodpecker mocked.

He leant down and his fingers hurried over the grass, here and there, looking for the cigarette-box. He found and opened it, taking out a cigarette. Again they set out to find the matches, which they found. He felt for the end that lit, he struck and heard the burst of flame. Fingers of the left hand groped down the cigarette in his mouth to the end, and he brought the match there. He puffed, he might have puffed anything then. He felt with a forefinger to see whether it was alight and he burned the tip. The match blew out with a shudder, and he threw it away.

How intolerable not to be able to smoke, but people said that you came to appreciate it in time, and it was degrading to chew gum. Was it still alight? Again he burned his finger. He threw the cigarette away. Now it would be starting a fire; still he had thrown it out on to the lawn. What was that? A tiny sound, miles away, no one but a blind man could possibly have caught it. He sniffed, he could smell the fire, very small yet, but starting, just one flame, invisible in the sunlight, eating a pine-needle. What was to be done? To leave it was madness, but how to find it to put it out? Await developments, there was nothing probably. Stevenson's last match.

All the same the cigarette was not burning anything, it was an invention typical of the country. He was getting into the country state of mind already, with no sense of proportion, and always looking for trouble. And he would become more and more like that, when one was blind there was no escape. It was a wretched business. The life of the century was in the towns, he had meant to go there to write books, and now he was imprisoned in a rudimentary part of life. And the nurse was busy nursing him back to a state of health sufficient for him to be left to their all-enfolding embrace of fatuity. So that all he could do to keep his brain a little his own was to write short stories. Perhaps one on the nurse, with her love of white wards and of stiff flowers, they were sure to be stiff if she had any, and of a ghastly antiseptic sanity. With her love of pain and horrors, and of interesting cases, with her devastating knowledge of human anatomy. But that was rather cheap, for she wasn't like that. She was merely dull, with a desire for something concrete and defined to hold on to. But she was dull.

He would write a story, all about tulips. That time when Mamma had taken him one Easter holidays to Holland, when the tulips had been out all along the railway line. And the cows with blankets on in case it rained. But no, it would have to be in England, the tourist effect in stories was dreadful. It would be a Dutchman with a strange passion for tulips – that was rather beautiful, that idea. Yes, and he would have passed all his life in sending tulips over to England, till he had come to think that England must have been a carpet of them in spring – he would have to be uneducated and think that England was only a very tiny island. He would be just a little bit queer with lovely haunting ideas that drifted through his brain, and he would love his tulips! So that Holland in springtime would not have enough tulips for him, and he would sell the little he had so as to buy a passage, that he might feed his soul on his tulips in England. His place in the bulb farm would be to address the wrappers, and there would be an address in Cumberland that he was told to write to very often. Then there would be those hills to work into the story, and he would go on a bicycle, which he had bought with his last penny, and each hill would seem to hide his tulips, they might be there, just beyond, behind the next hill. Till he would fall down, dead, his heart broken! But perhaps that was a little flat. It must simmer over in his brain. He would be very queer, with little fragments of insanity here and there. It would work.

The laziness of this afternoon.

Mrs Haye crushed grass on the way to Mrs Trench. Herbert stretched out a hand and made clucking noises, while Mrs Lane giggled. Weston shifted his feet slightly, and put his cap further back on his head, before the artichokes. Harry began hissing his way down another paragraph, and Doris was fondly tying a bow on the end of one pigtail. Jenny, the laundry cat, was two inches nearer the sparrow.

Nan put down her cup with a sigh and folded her hands on her lap, while her eyes fixed on the fly-paper over the table.

★　　★　　★

They were all standing round him on the lawn.

"Seven days old. I said what I could to Mrs Trench. A terrible affair. What can one do?"

"Poor little mite."

"What was it, Mrs Haye?"

"Gastric pneumonia, I think, nurse. I am sure that Brodwell muddled the case."

"To think of it!"

"Of course, Mrs Haye, gastric pneumonia with a seven days' child is very grave."

"Was it a boy or a little girl'm?"

"A girl. How is he to-day, nurse?"

"Oh, I'm all right."

"I think we are getting on very nicely, aren't we?"

"He has more colour to him to-day."

"Oh, Master John, you do look a heap better."

"Thanks, Nan, I'm sure I do."

"Yes, Mrs Haye, he really has. In one or two days we shall be up and about again, shan't we?"

"I suppose so."

"Of course you will, dear."

"It did give me a fright."

"Well, there's another fright over anyway, Nan."

"Dr Mulligan is not coming again, is he, nurse?"

"Only to-morrow, Mrs Haye, for a final inspection And I had perhaps be better getting ready to go back to town in a week or two, he is going on so quickly."

– Thank God, the woman was talkin' about goin'.

– Time she went, too, airified body.

"Well, nurse, I think in about ten days' time it will be safe for me to take over the dressings, and then there would be nothing left for you to do except teaching him how to get about and so on, and we can do that, can't we, Jennings?"

"We can do that'm."

Yes, they could do that. The nurse was intolerable, but at least she was alive, and now they were sending her away.

"Then, Mrs Haye, I can write up to town to tell them that I shall be free in, say, twelve days' time? That will make the 24th, won't it?"

"Yes, shall we say the 24th? Why, it's you, Ruffles. Oh, so old."

"Poor dog."

"How old is he, Mrs Haye?"

"Twelve years old. He ought to be destroyed. One must be practical."

"That's right. Kill him."

"But, my dear, it is cruel to let him live."

"He is too old to be healthy, Mrs Haye. They are germ traps."

Ruffles made confiding noises, wagging a patchy tail. An effluvia of decay arose.

"Perhaps it would be best."

78

It was a pity to shoot him, after he had been so good. How sentimental dogs were. Nan would be having one of her waves of silent grief. Their breathing descended in a chorus to where he lay, hoarse, sibilant, and tired. Were they thinking of Ruffles? Did they all snore at night?

The evening was falling away and the breeze had dropped. A midge bit him on the ankle and a drop of sweat tickled him by the bandages. The pigeons were all cooing together, there seemed to be no question and answer, they were in such a hurry to say everything that there wasn't time. Birds twittered happily and senselessly all round. Through it and over it all there was the evening calm, the wet air heavy everywhere. The sky would be in great form, being crude and vulgar.

They were silent because it was the evening, though they could not keep it up for long.

"A pretty sunset."

"It's that beautiful."

"I do love a sunset, Mrs Haye, I think . . ."

"A sunset, John" – the woman was intolerable.

"Ah."

"Is it not becoming a little fresh for him out here, Mrs Haye? We mustn't catch a chill."

"Perhaps. Jennin's, could you just go and tell William and Robert to come here to help Master John back."

"But I can walk by myself if one of you will give me their arm."

"I don't think we are quite strong enough yet, Mrs Haye."

She would write to-morrow to get her changed. It was too bad of them to send her this thing.

God blast the woman, why was he always treated as a baby? Oh, how they loved it, now that he was helpless.

"What time is it?"

"Eight o'clock, dear. Time for dinner. Ah, here are William and Robert."

Ruffles licked his hand. My only friend. Oh, he was sick and tired of it all.

"Now, dear, put your arm round William's shoulder, and the other round Robert . . ."

"Would it not be better, Mrs Haye, if between them they carried the chair and him on it?"

"Stairs – narrow. Now lift him. That's right. You can get along like that with them on each side, can't you, John?"

The woman was insufferable.

"Yes, I'm all right. Good-night, Ruffles."

"I'll come up and see you after dinner, dear."

William breathed discreetly but heavily, Robert full of energy. William's shoulders were thin.

"Mind, Master John, here's the step into the library."

The nurse walked quickly behind. Mrs Haye was a fool, and with no medical training, even if she were an honourable. Of course it was bad for the patient to walk upstairs. If she had had her way, they would never have put him in a room two storeys up, even if he had been in it since childhood. These ex-VAD's who gave themselves such airs.

Nan was drowned in a wave of silent grief.

To see him supported between Mr William and Robert with white bandages over his head and him so weak and feeble and who would never see again, and the nurse who was not fit to look after a sick boy she was that cantankerous.

She trailed away to a cup o' tea in the kitchen.

Mrs Haye went round to her sitting-room through the door in the wall of the rose garden. No solution yet, nothing found, nothing arranged. Only one or two letters of condolence left to answer. And the nurse was terrible. Terrible. The idea of carrying him up those narrow stairs. There might have been a nasty accident if the woman had had her way. And he was in such a difficult state of mind. You could not say a word to him without his taking it wrong.

Really, the only thing to do was to watch him and await developments. And in two or three years' time they would marry him to some nice girl, they would look out for one. There was – well, perhaps.

She went upstairs to dress for dinner.

He sat on a chair while the nurse got the bed ready. His head hurt him, the stairs must have done that. Poor Ruffles, it was too bad that he was finished. His head was throbbing; how he hated pain, and in the head it was unbearable. And this atmosphere of women. There was no male friend who would come to stay, he had always been too unpleasant, or had always tried to be clever, or in the movement. And now there was no escape, none. A long way away there might be a country of rest, made of ice, green in the depths, an ice that was not cold, a country to rest in. He would lie in the grotto where it was cool and where his head would be clear and light, and where there was nothing in the future, and nothing in the past. He would lie on the grass that was soft, and that had no ants and no bugs, and there would be no flies in the air and no sun above his head, but only a grey clearness in the sky, that stretched to mountains blue against the distance, through the door of his ice-house. There would be pine trees in clumps or suddenly alone, and strange little mounds, one after the other, that grew and grew in height till they met the mountains that cut off the sky. A country of opera-bouffe. And little men in scarlet and orange would come to fight up and down the little hills, some carrying flags, others water pistols. There would be no wounded and no dead, but they would be very serious.

Why couldn't there be something really romantic and laughable in life? With sentimentality and tuppenny realism. Something to wake one out of an existence like this, where day would follow day with nothing to break the monotony, where meal followed meal and where people sat still between meals letting troubles fall into their lap. Nothing stirred.

"There, it is ready now. Take off your dressing-gown and lean on my shoulder. There we are. Would you prefer to have your dressings renewed now, or after dinner?"

"Oh, now, to get it over."

He hated pain. He only half saw how pain fitted in with the scheme of things, and it made him afraid.

She was clinking bowls, and already the clean smell, far worse than any dung-heap, was all over the room.

Fingers began to unpin and to remove his bandages. It was hurting less to-day. No, it wasn't. Oh . . .

CHAPTER III

Picture Postcardism

In the green lane between Barwood and Huntly there was a stile in the tall hedge. Behind were laurels, and brambles, and box trees, and yews, all growing wild. At the end of a mossy path from the stile lay the house, built in yellow brick with mauve patterns, across a lawn of rank grass. It had been raised in 1840 by a Welshman, the date was over the door. But this was hardly visible, it was early morning and a heavy white mist smudged the outline. Birds were beginning to chatter, dawn was not far. There were no curtains to the house, and no blinds but one, torn, hanging askew across a dark window swinging loosely open on the ground floor. A few panes of glass were broken, and brown paper was stuck over the holes. There was a porch at the near end with most of the tiles off; they had been used to patch the roof, which was a dark blue-grey. At the far end was what had once been a hot-house, its glass broken.

The garden was dishevelled, no attempt had been made to clean it for many years, and the only sign of labour was the cabbages that Father, in a burst of energy, had planted in a former flower-bed. There was one huge beech tree, most beautifully tidy, and the only respectable member of the garden. The others merely went round the edge, keeping the chaotic growth from the neat meadows. The whole garden gave the effect of being unhappy because it had too much freedom. It was sad. And the house was sadder still with its wistful mauve patterns, looking so deserted and forlorn although it was lived in. Nobody loved it, and, though by nature so very feminine, it had to remain neuter and wretched. No one cared two farthings, and it felt that deeply. No one minded. The birds were chirruping heartlessly. From over the river the church struck a silver five.

At the back was a yard, in the middle a hen coop made out of an old army hut. A cock was crowing within, had been doing so for some time. There is a stable, with a rickety door off its lower hinge hanging ajar. A rat plays inside. There are holes in the red roof of the outhouse, gaping at the pink sky. Broken flagstones lie about, and weeds have grown through the cracks. The back door has lost its paint. The four windows stare vacantly with emptiness behind their leaded panes. The mist hangs sluggishly about, and the air is chill as the cock crows in his raucous tenor.

Then the sun lights up the top of the beech tree into golden fire, and there is a movement in the paleness. It begins to go, while the sky fades back into every-day life. The fire creeps down the beech till the tops of the overgrown laurels are alight, the mist has drawn off to the river just below there. Everything brightens and stretches out of sleep, the sky is blue almost. A butterfly aimlessly flutters over the cabbages, the flycatcher swoops down and she is swallowed; he was on guard already. A pigeon drives by, a bright streak of silver painted on him by the sun. The birds chirp in earnest as the sun climbs higher and begins to make shadows, while anywhere that a drop of dew catches the light he breaks into a gem. A gossamer web will dart suddenly across something, like a rainbow thread.

The chickens begin to make a great noise, scolding and crooning in their wooden prison, sounding very greedy. They want to be let out, for a late worm, who has come up to see the new day, may yet be left by the gobbling blackbirds and thrushes. The last mists are drawing out, a breeze is stirring, and the morning is crystal. The dew has made a spangled dress for everyone, and the weeds and straggling bushes are all under a canopy of brilliant drops of light.

84

A starling sits upon the chimney pot preening himself. A crow flies over the garden, glancing to right and left. The three yews are renewing their green in the sun, the laurels are shiny and clean. A rabbit hops out, looks round, and begins to nibble at the fresh grass, his last meal before he goes to bed.

The air is new.

All are one community, but it will not be for long. When the sun sucks up the dew and the moistness of the gossamer, everyone will be for himself again. Each bird will sing his own song, and not the song of the garden. "Me, me, me," he will say, "I am the best." And the nettles will whisper to each other, "You or me, you or me," laurels, yews, box trees and brambles too. Even the beech tree who has won to his great height and who has no rival in fifteen miles, he, too, will be straining, straining higher to the sun. It is all the sun, who has not climbed high enough yet.

The back door opened and she came out, pausing a moment before shutting the door behind her. She was tall and dressed in red slippers, a dirty blue serge skirt, and a thin, stale mauve bodice. She was so graceful! Her skin was unhealthy-looking, dark and puffed, her mouth small, the lips red. Her hair, black and in disorder, tangled down to her eyebrows. Across one cheek a red scar curved. Her eyes, a dark brown and very large, had a light that burned.

She felt alive, and she could see that the yard was dead – yes, she was like that this morning.

She stepped out into the yard, slammed the door behind her, and swept through the weeds that sprinkled her with dew. One big bramble twined so amorously round her skirt that her legs could not tear themselves free, and she had to bend to tear him off superbly. All over at the contact of her hands he trembled, and trembled there for some time. She went to the pump which stood near the outhouse, and the rat fled down his hole. She worked the pump handle till it chugged up water for her which she splashed over her face, wetting her dress as well. She went to the hen coop, opened the door, and stood waiting. The cock walked sedately out the first and she hurried him up with her carpet slipper, laughing to see him flustered. Her voice was deep, and, of course, had a coarse note in it. And then she went back into the house, all wet, banging the back door behind her.

Snores, deep and thick, came down from an open window above into the yard.

The cock was angry and he watched his hens for a moment with a sense of humiliation, one claw stopped in mid-air. He did not know but he felt out of sorts. Not in actual ill-health but liverish. All the same, if there was any-one to look at him they would see a fine sheen to his feathers to-day. He cried out to attract attention, and Natacha, who was by his side, said duteously that his ruff was stupefying in its beauty, rivalling the sun with its brightness. After it was all over, leaving Natacha squawking, he fluttered up on to the top of the coop. He was feeling ambitious, in revolt, the world was all wrong somehow, too soft, not enough dust for a dust-bath. There was not even a dung-heap in this wretched yard. Everything was too soft – the sun, and the dew, and the gentle weeds. He wanted heat, heat. Between intervals of killing things on himself he stretched out his neck and told this to the world, and that he was king of this castle.

Joan upstairs is putting on her stockings. What a lot of holes there are in them, but no matter. Sunday to-day. How will Father take the church bells? Last Sunday he had not minded very much. It is going to be beautifully hot, and Father will hate that too, poor old thing. George hated the heat, only she loved it. The wonderful sun!

How red her hands are getting, and rough. That was the house-work, while nice, young, rich ladies kept theirs folded with gloves on, and they had coloured umbrellas to keep the sun off. To be frightened of the sun! Nice young ladies had never done a day's work in their lives. Why should she work and they be idle? Oh, if she were like one of them! She would have light blue undies. Wouldn't she look a dream in the glass! And stays? No, no stays. But perhaps, they must fortify you so.

But what was the good of dreaming? – dreaming never did anyone any good. There was George, he might be working in the meadow to-morrow, and then she would lean over the stile – climb over the stile? – and talk to him, and get a few shy answers back, perhaps. George was wonderful, George was so exciting. With his fair hair, with his honey-coloured eyes, with his brick-red face so passion-ate, with his strength, with his smell. The one that drove the milk factory's lorry and that was always smoking a cigarette on his upper lip and that had that look in his eyes like a snake looking for his prey, she could not understand how she had seen anything in him. But George, with his honey-coloured ones, slow, but with it at the back of them, and with his shortness, and with his force, oh, it would, it must be something this time after such years of waiting. To find out all about it. "Yes, George, go on, go on."

What nice toes she had, except that the nails were rather dirty. But what was the good of keeping clean now? They weren't in the Vicarage any more, and there was no one to tell her how dirty or how pretty they were, except Father when he was drunk, but that, of course, did not count. George would say all that. She would teach him, if he didn't know.

She moves to a looking-glass and wrestles with her hair. In the glass was the brown-papered wall behind, the paper hanging in strips, showing the yellow plaster beneath. Those holes in the roof. And there was the rash that broke out in the top right-hand corner of the glass where the paint had come off the back. She was so miserable. The only chair has no back, and the front leg is rickety, so that you have to lean over to the right when you sit down. The bare boards of the floor are not clean, the bed-clothes are frowsy, the pillow greasy. Everything is going to go wrong to-day. It is close in here. She goes across the room and flings the window open.

By the window there was a small table, on it a looking-glass. She never used this one because you had to sit down to it, and that was tiresome. Draped round the oval frame and tied in wide, drooping bows to the two uprights was a broad white ribbon. Tied to the handles of the two drawers beneath were white bows also. On the low table were hair-brushes, a comb with three teeth out, a saucer full of pins and hairpins and safety pins and a medicine bottle, empty, with a bow round the neck made out of what had been left of the white ribbon. Violets, in a little bunch, lay by the bottle, dead.

She goes through the door into the next room, which is his. He is lying noisily asleep, with the bed-clothes half off his chest, and his red beard is spread greasily over the lead-white of his skin. One arm hangs down to the floor, the other, trying to follow it, is flung across his chest. His face has a nose, flat, hair red and skin blotchy. There is the usual homely smell of gin. The window was wide open to let out the snores.

And this was Father, Daddy, Daddums. Oh, he was pretty in bed. She couldn't remember him very well as he was at the Vicarage such ages ago, without his beard. It had been wonderful then: they had had a servant, which you could order about. And Mrs Haye, she used to terrify her, now she did not care two snaps of the finger although she had run away from her when she had seen her coming down the lane the other day; and Mrs Haye had called him Mr Entwhistle, the ordinary people, Passon, and Colonel Waterpower, whom they had met occasionally, had called him Padre. Silly all those people were with their silly ways, but they were so well dressed and the ladies too, those stuffs, so . . . And it was his fault that they were like this. You could see what people thought by their faces as they passed, they always went a little quicker when they caught sight of you coming. And they might still have been in the Vicarage.

Poor Father, perhaps it was not all his fault. And after all she was the only person left now to look after him. And the life wasn't too bad, he left her alone except when he was drunk and wanted someone to talk to. And he told her the most wonderful things. He was really a wonderful man, a genius. All it was, was that he was misunderstood. He saw visions and things. And really, in the end, it was all Mother's fault for being such a fool, though of course Father had been fond of gin before that. Mother, when she lay dying, with Father and her at the bedside, instead of whispering something she ought to have, had cried out quite loud *"John"* as if she was calling, right in front of the doctor and the village nurse and that. Then she was dead, and they were her last words. John was still the postman. She had been a fool, and Father had drunk much more gin ever afterwards. After Mother died Father had been unfrocked, that was soon after the beginning of the war, partly for the gin, and partly for the talk about Mother. Mr Davies died in time, and with most of the money that Uncle Jim had left them when he was killed they had bought this house here, only two miles away. It would have been nicer to go somewhere new, but as Father said, "he was not going to run away from those that had hounded him from the parish."

What was she doing standing still? She had to wake him and then get breakfast and then clear up. "Here, wake up. Wake up," and she picks up the clothes, flung anyhow on the floor, and smooths them, putting them at the foot of the bed. Roses on wallpaper, roses hung down in strips from the damp wall pointing. "Get up, get up." He was shamming, that he might give her more work to do. Yes, that was it. "Do you hear? Get up." She lifts his white shoulders and shakes him till the blue watery eyes open.

She lets him flop back on to the pillow, the red finger-marks on his skin fading away again.

His eyes open painfully. He scratches, gazing vacantly at the ceiling.

"Another day?"

"Yes."

"Oh."

"I'll go and get you some water, if you'll get up."

"Well, go and get it then."

She goes to the pump, and he drags himself out of bed. He is short and thick-set, with bulging flesh. He has been sleeping in an old pair of flannel trousers. He sits on a box by the window. He looks out beyond the garden, over the meadow and the quiet river, to where the trees cover a hill on the other side. Their green dresses are blurred by the delicate blue mist that swims softly round them, the deep shade yawns the sleep away. In the meadows some cows lie in the open, it is not hot enough yet to drive them under the hedges. Below, a hen chuckles with satisfaction. How quiet it all was, nothing wrong in the best of all possible worlds. They thought that, all the rest of them, they did not care. And he was forgotten. Nature insulted him. What right had the country to look like this, basking in the sunshine while he lived in the middle of it? He with his great thoughts, his great sufferings. Why didn't the State support him, instead of letting him live in squalor? He deserved as much of the money from the bloated capitalist as anyone else. It was their class that had brought him to this, they had never paid him enough, for one thing. It was their fault. Where was the water?

To-day was going to go badly, it was going to be terribly hot. Sunday too, so that the church bells would ring and then he would remember Barwood church, the little altar, the roses – his roses – growing outside. He felt so ill to-day, not at all strong. He would weep when the bells rang, weep because so many things were over, the Colonel calling him

90

Padre, the deference of the churchwarden. How great his tears would be. All that was so far and yet so close. Every day he thought it over. But there was no need to regret it, he was working out his salvation here, if he had stayed on in that Vicarage he would have been dead alive. He was so vital here, and then somehow the grasp of it would leave him.

He was ill to-day all the same, he felt it inside, something seriously the matter. Was it the cancer? There, turning over and over. Yes, there it was. Here; no, there; no, no, there. Yes. Cancer, that he had been awaiting so long.

"Here's the water."

He winced. The noise the girl made. Was he not ill?

"I am ill."

"Again?"

"It's the cancer at last."

There was a certain satisfaction now that it had come.

"Again. The doctor will cost you a bottle just for telling you it's imagination. I know them and you."

"Go away, go away."

She was essentially small in character, like that mistaken woman her mother. Oh, he couldn't any more. Cancer coming on top of it all. What a fine tragedy his was. And it would cut short his great work, before even it had been begun.

She opened the door downstairs and went into the kitchen. He was much the same to-day, a little stronger perhaps, but that would go till he stoked up in the evening. Poor, weak creature.

Through a small window in a small bay looking out on to the garden the sunlight comes in and washes the dirt off the worn, red tiles. There is a sour smell of old food, and underneath the two windows on the right lie some empty sardine tins which have missed the gaps in the glass when thrown away. She goes to the cupboard, which is on the left. On it is an almanack from the ironmonger in Norbury, ten years old, with a picture in the middle of a destroyer cutting rigid water shavings in the sea, with smoke hurrying frozenly out of its funnels, and with a torpedo caught into eternity while leaping playfully at its side, out of the water and into the air. She jerks the cupboard open. Inside are plates, knives and forks, cups, and a teapot, all in some way chipped or broken. There are tinned foods of every kind, most of all sardines, and three loaves. At the bottom are two pails and a mangy scrubbing-brush and some empty gin bottles. On the top shelf some unopened bottles and a few cakes of soap are jumbled up with vaguely folded sheets and towels. She takes out a sardine tin and a loaf of bread and pitches them with two knives on to the table in the middle of the room. A chunk of butter on half a plate she puts down, as well as two cups without handles, and the milk-holding teapot. He has an injured spout, poor thing.

She goes over to the bay window and flings it open. She rolls up the torn blind. Father liked going round at night occasionally, "shutting up" as if he lived in a castle, but as he could never see straight enough by then to find the window latches it was not much good, but he always pulled down the blind. The range was disused and rusty, it had not been lighted since April. Before it was a tub of greasy water in which she did the washing up. The sun did not get far into the room. The paper here also was beginning to peel from the walls. An early bluebottle buzzed somewhere.

There was a movement in the sunlight, a scamper, and Minnie was arching his back against her leg, while his tail waved carefully at the end. Minnie, so fresh, so clean, the darling. Cat's eyes looked up at her, yellow and black. "Minnie, have you killed anything?" In a rush he was out of the window – how like darling Minnie – his tail a pennant. Then he is back, the clever darling, and in his mouth a dead robin redbreast. How he understood. "Oh, Minnie, the little sweet. Look at his crimson waistcoat and his crimson blood. Why, he is still warm. Shall we give him to

Father for his breakfast? What a clever Minnie," and Minnie purrs half attention. He paddles a paw in a speck of blood. She bends down, taking him in her arms. "Oh, Minnie, what a clever Minnie." But with a light jump he was out of her arms and was going to the window, and then was out of it. Joan follows, looks out, and Minnie is standing there, quite still, detached. Then he was off, slipping by everything, while the dew caught at his coat. How lovely cats were, she adored her Minnie.

A slow step came down the stairs, with a careful pause at the hole on the ninth step from the ground, and he comes in shakily. His face is baggy and fallen in, his black clothes have stains. He is wearing a dirty drainpipe collar, for it is the Sabbath, while round it a khaki shirt flaunts, without the black dicky. He stands in the doorway, his beard waggling.

"Sardines? Again? I tell you I can't eat them."

"We ought to be glad to eat what is given to us."

"Don't throw up quotations like that at me just to annoy me. Do you hear? Given, who said it was given? I paid for it, didn't I? You hate me, and everyone hates me."

But that was as it should be, he ought to take a pride in the hatred of the world. It was ever so with the great. But sardines, he paid for them. There had been a time when he had thanked God for sardines, because he had always hated them so that he saw in them his cross. But what was the good? He paid for them, and ate them because it was better than eating dry bread. After all he had paid for them, and if he had not paid he would not have got them, so where did thanks come in? He ought only to thank that oil-well in Southern Texas where Hoyner the cinema-man came from. There had been a time when he had thanked God for oil-wells, wars and apples, while these were nothing but unfortunate mistakes, he having lost half his money in Mexican oil, and apples being bad for his digestion. Why did he keep that money in oil? – it would go like the other half had. But it was so awkward changing. It was all so difficult. But then if no one ate fish the industry would die and with it the fishermen. No, thank God, he could see nothing divine in anything now, whereas in the old days he had eaten even a sardine with considerable emotion. Yet how could one be sure? His reason, how it tortured him, how it pursued round and round, coldly, in his brain. He had a fine intellect, too. Edward had told him that thirty years ago at Oxford. And it had been growing, growing ever since in his hermit existence, even Joan could not deny it . . . He was even more of a genius because he was recognised in his home, a very rare thing surely. And his reward would come, it must come. Yes, he would start work this very morning. But he felt so ill, weak.

"I feel so ill this morning, child. I have such a headache. And I am so weak" – physically only, of course; no, not mentally.

"Have a drop of gin in your milk. That will make it all right."

"Yes, I think you are right" – but no more than one, really.

He was always like that before the morning one. Poor Father.

That is better, more comfortable. But still there may be something wrong with him. He swallows another gin-and-milk.

"It's the cancer, Joan, that's what I am so terrified about. I can feel it glowing hot. We can't afford an operation or morphia. I shall die."

It would be nice to die; but no, it wouldn't be, and that was very unreasonable. But no, it wasn't, there was his book.

He was so clever that he had always been bottom at school – all great men had been bottom at school. Then he had lost his way in the world. No, that wasn't true, he had found it – this, this gin was his triumph. It was the only thing that did his health any good, and one had to be in good spirits if he was to think out the book, the great book that was to link everything into a circle and that would bring him recognition at last, perhaps even a letter from the Bishop. It would justify his taking something now and again as he did. But one doubted, there were days when one could not see it at all. How ill he felt. Some deep-seated disorder. How dreadful a disease, cancer. Why could not the doctors do something about it? Oh, for a pulpit to say it from.

Terrible, terrible.

"Father, where did you put the tin-opener for these sardines?"

"I don't know. My pain. Never had it."

"But it must be somewhere. It isn't in the cupboard here."

"Can't you open it with a fork? It's all laziness. Why bother me? Oh, here it is in my pocket. How funny."

"You are drinking all the gin. No, look here, you mustn't have any more. There will be none for this evening at this rate."

"But I'm not going to drink any more, I tell you. Leave me alone."

"Oh, yes. Here, give me that bottle."

"I shan't; I want it, I tell you. My health."

"Give it me."

You could be firm with him in the morning. She locks up the bottle in the cupboard, slips the key inside her dress, and begins to open the sardines. He is almost in tears, "insulted, by a girl, my daughter. When it was for the good of my health, as I was ill." But he wasn't such a fool, oh no. He had a dozen beneath the floor of the study. He had wanted to drink more lately, and the girl always regulated his bottle a day carefully.

"Damn, I've cut myself with the tin-opener."

There is a gash in her thumb, and she bleeds into the oil which floats over the sardines. Serve her right, now she

95

would get blood-poisoning, her hand would swell and go purple, and it would hurt. They would die in agony together. Think of the headlines in the evening papers, the world would hear of him at last: "AMAZING DISCOVERY IN LONELY COTTAGE," then lower down, "UNFROCKED GENIUS AND HIS BEAUTIFUL DAUGHTER FOUND DEAD." Beautiful. Was she? Yes, of course she was, as good as anyone's daughter anyway, except for the scar. The scar, it was like a bad dream, he had a hazy memory of her taunting him, of his throwing the bottle and missing, and of throwing one of the broken bits, and of catching her with it on the cheek. It was horrible. Still it was what a genius would have done. He was so weak this morning. What was he thinking about? Yes, suicide, and the headlines in the papers. But in any case it would be over in three days. What was the use of it all? And what was he eating, blood-stained sardine? He did feel sick. Cancer.

She had bound up her finger in a handkerchief, and was eating sardines on slabs of bread-and-butter, heads and tails, while he unconsciously cut these off. She eats with quick hunger, her chin is greasy with the oil coming from the corners of her mouth. She says thickly:

"I love sardines, and the oil is the best thing about them."

No answer.

Poor Father, he was in for a bad day, for it was going to be very hot, and he must have had a bad night, he was a little worse than usual. And he did hate sardines so, but there was nothing else to eat, except the kipper in tomato sauce, and they were going to have a tin of that for lunch. Father was really not very well, perhaps this talk of cancer wasn't all nonsense. But it must only be the drink. He was such a nasty sight, with his finicky tastes and his jumpy ways. Think if George were there across the table, eating with a strong appetite, with his strong, dirty nails, the skin half grown over them, instead of Father's white ones, the last thing about himself that he spent any trouble over. They were one of his ways of passing the time, while she slaved. There would be something behind his honey-coloured eyes, a strong hard light, instead of blue wandering, weak ones. His face would be brick-red with the sun, his flesh inside the open shirt collar – there would be no starch about him – would be gold with a blue vein here and there; he would be so strong, it would be wonderful to be so frightened of him. Gold. While that weak creature over there, why even his beard was bedraggled and had lost its colour. Yet there were times when his body filled out and his voice grew, and when his beard flamed. Her fingers crept to the scar on her cheek, it had been wonderful that night. You felt a slave, a beaten slave.

But it was the scar that frightened George. His eyes would stray to the scar and look at it distrustfully; at first he had looked at her dress with horror, but she had not made that mistake again. Still he never spoke, which was so annoying, but lately there had been more confidence and shrewdness in his eyes. But the others did use to say something, all except Jim, he had been worse than George. Of course, no one ever saw her with him, it would scare him if the village began to talk. But it was very exciting. It was incredible to think how the days had passed without him.

There were now two bluebottles busy round the head of a sardine about three days old. The head lay there, jagged at the neck where Father had pulled off the body, a dull glaze over the silver scales, the eyes were metallic. There was blue on the two bluebottles who never seemed content, they buzzed up and down again so. Minnie had come in by the little bay window, and the bluebottles seethed with anger at being disturbed by someone besides themselves.

She rises sideways without stirring her chair, whispering hoarsely:

"Minnie, Minnie, come here."

But he slips by her hands. The key slipped down her leg to tinkle on the floor.

"That cat. Ah you, go away, go away," and he gets up, his chair screeching along the red tiles. He throws his knife feebly, it misses Minnie and makes a clatter. He is out of the window in a flash, and Father sits down again. She puts the key under the bread.

"I do hate cats, they frighten me so. There is something so dreadful about a cat, the way she seems to be looking at nothing. They don't see flesh and blood, they see an abstract of everything. It's horrible, horrible. Joan, you might keep her away from me, you know how I hate her. I can't bear any cat. And in my condition. I think you might, yes, I do think you might."

"All right, but I don't see what you mean. Minnie is such a darling, I don't know why you hate her."

"Of course you don't know cats as they really are. He is a devil, that cat."

Poor Father.

Outside, on the right, a hen stalks reflectively, her head just over the weeds. Her eye is fixed, its stare is irritating, and the way she has of tilting her head to look for food is particularly precious. She goes forward slowly, often dipping out of sight to peck at something. All that can be seen of her is a dusty-brown colour, dull beside the fresh green round her, encouraged by the sun into a show of newness. He watches her one visible eye with irritation.

"A chicken, at six in the morning, and loose in the garden. That shouldn't be. A pen. I will build a pen for them some time. I will start to-day, but then there is no rabbit wire, and we can't afford wire." Yet hens in one's garden. Degrading. Yet why not? They had to live, it was only fair to them that he should let them get food even if they were in his way, because they gave him food, and he did not deserve it. All the same, he did. And they were

God's creatures, even if they did come out of an egg, and even more because they did so. But was that true? No. Yes. He couldn't see at all to-day. Scientists understood the egg, all except the life that entered it – and that was God; there, there you are. But an *egg*. He didn't know. There was something. He did not know. No, not in an egg.

He gets up and moves towards the door by the cupboard.

"You'll never build that pen, and you know it. Here, what are you going to the Gin Room for?"

"Don't use that tone to me. Can't your Father go where he likes? Can't he retire to his study for a little peace? You seem to have no – no feeling for your Father."

And he was gone. That meant he had some gin in there, but you couldn't help it, there was nothing to be done, and he was better when he had drunk a little, he was more of a Man. And what was the use of worrying? and anyway it pulled him together. Blast this finger, why had she been such a fool as to jab it open? It hurt too, though not very much, still it would have been nice to have had someone to be sorry about it and to help her tie it up. If George had been here she would have been able to make such a lot of it. Those bluebottles, there were three of them round that sardine now, and three more over there, all in the sun. That was the one sensible thing about them; how she loved the sun. She put the key into the table drawer.

★   ★   ★

The clock in the village church across the fields struck twelve in a thin copper tenor that came flatly through the simmering heat. No bird sang, no breath of air stirred, nothing moved under the sun who was drawing the life out of everything except Joan. She got up slowly, damp with sweat, from the window-sill where she had been stewing in the white light. The wood of it was unbearably hot, and what few traces of paint that were left, blistered. She fanned

99

herself with the old straw hat she had been wearing, and tried to make up her mind to go out and find the eggs for dinner. She loved the sun, he took hold of you and drew you out of yourself so that you couldn't think, you just gave yourself up. She loved being with him all round her till she couldn't bear it any more. You forgot everything except him, yet you could not look up at him, he was so bright. He was so strong that you had to guard your head lest he should get in there as well. He was cruel, like George. And he was stronger than George, but then George was a Man.

The air, heavy with the wet heat, hung lifeless save when her straw hat churned it lazily into dull movement. Three bluebottles, fanning themselves angrily with their wings at the windows, by their buzzing kept the room alive. She was lost in a sea of nothingness, and all the room too. From inside Father's room came low moans at intervals, the heat had invaded and had conquered Father. Oh, it is hot, she is pouring with sweat all over, and her hands feel big and clumsy and heavy with blood, there is nowhere to put them. How cool the iron range is, its fireplace gazing emptily up the chimney at the clean blue of the sky. Her hand on the oven door leaves a moist mark which vanishes slowly.

She must look for eggs, though how the poor hens can lay in this weather she didn't know. Think of having feathers, dusty feathers on you for clothes on a day like this. And laying eggs. Minnie would be hot too, in an impersonal sort of way. But the poor hens. Why they would die of it, poor darlings, and the old cock, the old Turk in his harem, what would happen to him, how would he keep his dignity? She would have to go and look, besides she was sticky all over, and it would be cooler moving about.

She leaves the kitchen and goes round to the back under the arch in the brick wall that went to the outhouse, and up which a tortured pear tree sprawled, dead, and so into the yard. The stench is violent, and with the sun beating down she drifts across to the pump, limp as if she has forgotten how alive she had thought she was. She works the handle of the pump slowly till the water gushes reluctantly out. Then she splashes it over her face as it falls into the stone trough, and she plunges in her heavy hands – how nice water was, so cool, so slim, and she would like to be slim, like you saw in fashion plates in the papers, ladies intimately wrapped in long coats that clung to their slimness, they drank tea and she milk; Father said the water was unsafe, although it was so clear and pure and cool. It was hot.

The cock was lost in immobility in the shade of the stable, and she had forgotten about him.

She went round the side of the house, past the window of Father's room till at the corner she came to the conservatory, the winter garden, inside which the crazy hen sometimes laid. She was crazy because she would cry aloud for hours on end and Joan never knew why, though perhaps it was for a chick that a fox had carried off once. The broken glass about caught the sun and seemed to be alight, and inside it was a furnace. Standing quite still in a corner was the hen, but no egg. She was black, and quite, quite still.

In front the beech tree kept a cave of dark light, behind and on each side the tangled bushes did the same, each kept his own, and the giant uneven hedge. They were all trying to sleep through it. She ploughs through the grass and looks vaguely here and there, into the usual nests and the most likely places. Under an old laurel tree with leaves like oil-cloth, into an arching tuft of grass. A bramble lies in wait, but she brushes him aside. Two or three flies come after her, busy doing nothing. She passes by clouds of dancing grey gnats in the shade.

Still no eggs.

Nothing of course under the yew, so old that he empoisoned and frightened young things. Drops of sweat fell down. Here was the box tree who kept such a deep shade. There were two eggs. She turns, and crossing a path of sunlight, enters the shade of the beech and sits down, her back against his trunk. If he were George.

She thinks of nothing.

Then she finds that the house is ugly, the yellow and mauve answer back so coldly to the sun. And it was so small and tumble-down. The life was so full, so bitter. If she could change it. There would be the long drive through the great big park with the high wall round it and the great big entrance gates, made of hundreds of crowns in polished copper. After that you would come suddenly through a wood of tall poplars upon a house that was the most beautiful in the world, made of a lot of grey stone. Standing on the steps to greet her as she steps out of her luxurious car would be the many footmen dressed in scarlet, and all young and good-looking. Inside would be the huge staircase, and the great big rooms furnished richly. On a sofa, smoking a cigar, would be the husband, so beautiful. He would have lovely red lips and great big black eyes. Like a sort of fairy story. It would be just like that.

But there was the other dream. A small house with a cross somewhere to show it was a vicarage, and a young clergyman, her husband, and lots and lots of children. She would be in the middle, so happy, her big dark eyes shining like stars, and they would be stretching out chubby fingers to her. But what was the good of dreaming? – dreaming never did anyone any good.

It was nicer to live as you were, and George might be somewhere near. There were the eggs to do.

She wriggles round and looks out, through the gap with the little gate, over the river sunk in her banks and invisible, to the trees on the hill that were soaked in blue, with sunshades of bright sun green on top. A pigeon moves, winking grey, through them; no sound breaks the quiet. It is a sleepy blue, and how the ground was bubbling, air bubbles rising that you could see. She would have to go and boil the eggs, and bubbles would come then. The oil lamp would make such a heavy smell. She liked them raw, but Father would have them boiled. It had to be done. Father was a great baby, and he had to be fed.

She gets up and moves slowly into the house without bothering to put on her straw hat again. From the cupboard underneath the stairs she takes out the lamp with a saucepan fixed above it and carries it into the kitchen. She fills the saucepan by dipping it into the washing-up water, and puts the two eggs in, then lights the lamp with a match from the box on the shelf over the range. Bubbles very soon appear mysteriously from nowhere in the water, and these grow more and more, till the eggs move uneasily at the number of them. Eggs, why do chickens come out of eggs? It was like a conjuring trick, darling little yellow woolly, fluffy things who were always hurrying into trouble! But she knew just how the hen felt with them, it would be wonderful. How long had they been in? Oh dear, the heat and the smell! Poor eggs, it was rather hard on them. This must be about right, and she turns the flame off. Now for the bread and kippers in tomato sauce and plates and spoons and cups and – the milk, she had forgotten the milk. And she could not go to Mrs Donner's, it was too hot. Father would have to drink gin, he wouldn't mind, but she would, she hated it. She went to the door of his room and beat upon it with the palm of her hand, leaving damp marks wherever she touched it. "Father dinner is ready." His voice answered, "All right." It was weary, but with a stronger note.

He shambles into the room dejectedly.

"Oh, it is hot, it is hot."

"Yes. Father, here's an egg."

"Thank you. Oh dear."

They begin to eat, he carefully, and she roughly. He takes up his cup to drink.

"Milk."

"There isn't any left."

"No milk? Why is there no milk? We always drink milk

at lunch, don't we? And Mrs Donner always has milk, doesn't she? Why is there no milk?"

"You know we can't afford it."

"I don't suppose we can, but can't I have a little luxury occasionally, with my bad health?"

"I don't know."

"You don't know, and what's more, you don't care, you don't mind that you make your poor old Father uncomfortable. Where would you have been without me? . . . Don't smile, shut that smile or I'll knock it inside out." He is streaming with sweat, it falls in blobs on to the table. She just didn't care, didn't care. He'd make her care soon enough. But what was it all for?

"Any gin left for me?"

"Don't taunt me, don't taunt me, don't taunt me . . . don't . . ." and his voice rises, and his face crinkles into funny lines. She was taunting him, taunting him. Just when he felt so ill, too. He did feel ill. And these rows were so thin. Ill.

He gets up and goes to the door of his room, dragging his feet.

"Where are you going? More gin?"

"Yes, more gin. Why shouldn't I? Just one more."

"But aren't you going to finish your egg? – and then there's the nice kipper and tomato sauce."

"I tell you I can't eat, I'm ill," and he pulls to the door of his room.

Silly old Father, he was ridiculous, and yet it must be horrid to be as unhappy as all that. Anyway, it would mean all the more for her. She finishes his egg and then opens and begins to eat the fish. She does not eat prettily. He is having no lunch. Is he really ill? No, it was the gin. Still, it was her job to look after him, if she didn't who would? And if he was ill and died she would feel just like the hen who trod to death a chick – yes, just like that. For he was hers, he was an awful child, and he had to be looked after, and he had to be petted when he cried. He had to be told how wonderful he was, and if you told him he was a genius he would at once cheer up and begin talking about birds and trees, and the sky and the stars. There was something queer about stars, they were mysterious, like Minnie's eyes, only nice and small; and she liked nice small things, when she saw them. They were cool too. There were heaps of things she did like, but then she didn't have the time, she was so busy. What was a genius exactly? How hot it was, and she wanted a drink.

★　　★　　★

Everything was old and sleepy. The sun, who was getting very red, played at painting long shadows in the grass. The air was tired and dust had risen from nowhere to dry up the trees. Sometimes a gentle little breath of wind would come up moving everything softly, and a bird would sing to it perhaps. All was quiet. Gnats jigged. From over the river the clock struck a mellow golden eight. The sun began throwing splashes of gold on to the trees, even the house caught some and was proud to be under the same spell.

The air began to get rid of the heaviness, and so became fresher as the dew soaked the grass. A blackbird thought aloud of bed, and was followed by another and then another. The sun was flooding the sky in waves of colour while he grew redder and redder in the west, the trees were a red gold too where he caught them. The sky was enjoying herself after the boredom of being blue all day. She was putting on and rejecting yellow for gold, gold for red, then red for deeper reds, while the blue that lay overhead was green.

A cloud of starlings flew by to roost with a quick rush of wings, and sleepy rooks cawed. Far away a man whistled on his way home.

Joan came from the porch as the light failed and moved

peacefully to the gate. She went through and crossed the meadow, the heavy grass dragging at her feet. Some cows ate busily near by and hardly bothered to look up. Then the river flowing mysteriously along with the sky mirrored in the varnished surface. Trailing willows made light smiles at the sides where the water was liquid ebony. An oily rise showed a fish having an evening meal. He was killing black flies. Joan sat on the bank.

Opposite, between sky and water, a fisherman is bent motionless over his float. He never moves except to jerk violently at times. Then, a short unseen struggle, a bending rod, and another fish to die. Joan thinks he must be a clever fisherman to catch so many fish, but it is silly to trouble about him while there is George to think of. Why, he has caught another, it is a big one too, it is taking quite a time to land. The reel screams suddenly like someone in pain, he must be a big fish. The little bent figure gets up and begins to dance excitedly about. A plunge with the landing-net, a tiny tenor laugh of pleasure, and then peace again as he leans over the net, doing things.

George, what if George were here now? He would say nothing but would merely sit, his great idle form. And then . . . yes.

The blackbirds had stopped. Blue shadows had given way to black. The little man was taking down his rod, and soon had gone off into the dusk on a bicycle, dying fish in his creel. There was the moon, reserved and pale but almost full. How funny to go up the sky, then down again. Aah. She was sleepy, yawning like that. And it was getting cold sitting out here. The river was ebony, and away in the west was a bar of dying purple across the sky. The trees had vast, unformed bulks. The moon shed a sickly light round her on a few clouds that had come up all at once. It was cold. She jumped up and began to walk back to the house. But she would not go to bed yet.

Yes, there was the light in his room, a candle flame, still.

She closed the door carefully behind her and crept upstairs in the dark. The hole on the third step and the creaking board on the ninth, she passed both without making a noise. Then through his room into hers and she was safe. She jammed her door with the chest of drawers, a heavy thing which she moved easily, it had the four castors intact for some reason. Funny how some of the furniture kept up appearances. Old days almost. Below it was quiet. She sat on a box in the window, and the cool night air breathed gently in, softly, like a thief.

Barwood . . . no, why think of that place? Everything had been so cultured there and so nice, and now it had all been beaten out of her, so that it hurt to go back into it. If there hadn't been any milk left for lunch you had sent for it and it came, you didn't have to pay for it on the nail as you did now. And she had been so clean and pretty, it was filthy here, but that had gone, and there was only the memory of it to go back to. Not that they hadn't always let her run wild, though. But things had changed since then, Mother wouldn't know her again if she could see her now . . . Barwood Vicarage had been one of those houses that have white under the roof. An old wall went round. Little trees grew out of the wall, and their roots made cracks in it. One thick arm of ivy worked its way through just before the gate and made a bulge in the top. There was an old lawn and a gardener who looked much older, but then he can't have been. It was a deep green, and he mowed it lovingly twice a week with a scythe, he was so proud of his mowing, and it used to be such fun going up to him and saying how well he did it, to watch new wrinkles come out with his smile. His face always looked as if there could be no more wrinkles, and yet there were new ones. Swallows used to build under the roof and then used to show off, they flew so fast and so close. For hours she had watched them rush in a swoop to the door of the nest. They never missed.

The only party at Barwood, the huge lawn and the

107

immense house, the footman in livery, the people, it was another world. There had been ladies on the lawn dressed in marvellous stuffs with brightly-coloured hats – like birds they were. They shook hands very nicely and kindly, then they rushed away to play before the men. Mother had sat talking to Mrs Haye, with her on the other side, and Mother had laid a restraining hand on her all the time as she half bent over Mrs Haye. The unhappiness of that afternoon. Who were these people who lived such beautifully easy lives, and what right had they to make you so uncomfortable? The men were such willing idols. A little boy, Hugh his name had been, had sat next her for a time, sent by his mother. He was at school then. He had asked her if she had been to the Pringles' dance, and she had blushed – silly little fool – when she had said no. Then he had said something was "awfully ripping," how at ease he had seemed, and then his glancing blue eyes had fixed and he had gone off and soon was laughing happily with an orange hat. Yes, he had left her for that thing, but you couldn't blame him. How cool they all were, even when hot after tennis; Mother's hand had been hot, lying in the lap of her new muslin which Mother had made for her. It might have been yesterday. That hand had seemed to be between her and the rest. Tennis was a pretty game to watch, and the men had laughed so nicely at it, with their open collars. One had had a stud-mark on his skin where the stud had pressed. Then there had been cool drinks on a sideboard – everything was new. Sometimes one of the ladies would say something to her with a quarter of her attention, the rest of her watching the men, and she herself had been too shy to answer . . . She had had a little ear under a kiss-curl, that lady. Mother still talked to Mrs Haye. People would sometimes look at the three of them seated on the bench, and then they would look away again and laugh. Oh, she hated them, it was their sort that had brought them to this. Sitting on the bench there she had begun to long for the tiny lawn and the poor

108

old broken dolly. A dream, those beautifully-dressed people who had been so cool, and whom mother had been so frightened at. Then they had gone, and she had had to say good-bye to Mrs Haye – "What a fine upstandin' girl, Mrs Entwhistle" – and they had begun to walk the mile home. What a little fool she must have made of herself that afternoon. Mother had been so funny, she remembered her so well saying eagerly, "Did you see the green dress that girl with the auburn hair was wearing? And the white one of the girl with the thick ankles?" That had been the first time they had talked dresses as if it was not Mother who bought hers without asking her opinion. That night she had dreamed of a wonderful party with Hugh and his blue eyes and fat cheeks, when he had been terribly nice to her, and when they had had the sideboard to themselves. But behind it all lay the memory of the preparation, her hair being brushed endlessly, her longing to be off and her longing to stay behind, the interminable delays and the too short walk. "Behave nicely, and for heaven's sake don't bite your nails."

And the dolly. Thomas, the old gardener, used to say, "Bean't she a beauty!" as he leant on his spade as Dolly was shown to him every day. He never said more than that, it was enough. Then there had been the time when she had dropped her, and one arm had come off, just as any grown-up's might. Fool, fool. She had cried for ages, and had given up all interest in her for a time because she had cried so much. But she went back to her, and Father glued on the arm so that it came off again; still they made it up and between them settled that she should have only one arm.

Then there had been Father's roses. They bordered the path from the drawing-room French window to the door in the wall. Just over it climbing roses scrambled up and hung down in clusters. And little rose trees stood out on each side of the path, and red and white roses peeped out from the green leaves that hid the thorns. Father was so proud of them, ever since she could remember he used to talk about them at tea. He planted more and more, till the vegetable garden was invaded and in the end was a jungle of roses. His duties had to wait while they were being sprayed, or pruned, or manured. Thomas, of course, was never allowed to touch, it was his grief, he longed to help look after them. She remembered him saying wistfully, "Them be lovely roses, Miss Joan." Roses, roses, all the way. Ro – o – ses.

There had been another side to the roses. She could remember the quarrels Mother used to have with him over them as if it was yesterday. The manure – best fish manure – cost money, and she would tell Father, in that funny high voice of hers that she used when she was angry, that one or the other would have to go, and then the rest was always whispered, sometimes less, sometimes more, but it must have been the gin or the roses. Father had not minded, nor had Mother after a time. John, the postman, must have begun about then. It was a pretty uniform. So it had gone on.

Mrs Haye complained that Father never visited until they were dead. Of course he had visited. And the Parochial Church Council had asked for more services, though, of course, no one ever came to church, only Mrs Haye, and she merely as an example to the village. The almshouse people came, but only because they were so nearly dead. The almshouses were built in dark blue brick, always in half-mourning, among the tombstones. Father had told her about these complaints over the rose trees. He had talked a great deal to her then. Poor Father. So he had planted roses to climb up the church, and they had given him a new interest there till Mrs Haye had made him pull them down. He had been running away.

There had been a queer light at the back of Mother's eyes about then – how she understood that light now! At the same time Mother had stopped taking any notice and would only smile tiredly at the things that had made her angry before. She took to painting her lips, and sometimes she would put one of the roses in her hair. Father never said anything about it to *her*, only, lying in bed with the owls hooting, she used to hear quarrels going on, quite often. Bed meant owls then, there were none here. He spent more and more time on the roses about the house. And in the summer he would dream himself away among them, sitting there by the hour while she played on the lawn, putting Dolly to bed in rose petals. Would it do if she painted her lips for George? No, it would frighten him. To-morrow was Monday, he might be about. They had been all right, too, when they had blossomed, great bunches of them, red and white, all over the place. Just like those beautiful picture postcards Mrs Donner had in the window sometimes. They had been lovely, those days.

Joined on to the Vicarage behind there had been a small house with a farmyard and a few buildings. It was the lower farm of Mr Walker's. Henry had lived in the house, Henry who was her first love. They had kissed underneath the big thistle in the orchard hedge, only he had been rather dirty. She had seen him driving a cart two weeks ago, only he had looked the other way. Didn't like to own her now. Before he had always lifted his cap with a knowing smile. Or had he been sorry for her? How funny that first kiss was. She had only been fourteen. All wet. But he remembered. Mrs Baxter, his mother, with her nice face and her chickens. Mrs Baxter used to come in sometimes to help Mother with the housework. She always used to say, "God is good to us, Mr Entwhistle," when Father was about. And Father used to look serious and say, "Yes, Mrs Baxter. He is indeed." He was, then. She used to call her "Miss."

Then the Wesleyan, "the heretic," had started a rival Sunday school. He gave a treat once a year and Father never did, so all the children went to him and left Father. He had been angry: "Bribery and corruption; I won't bribe the children to come to God." Then they could not afford to give tea at the Mothers' Meetings, and Mother had lost her temper with Mrs Walker, who had insinuated that they were lazy. But the real reason why no one came any more must have been the gossip about Father which began about then. But they had become indifferent; they hadn't cared.

Mrs Haye had called and had stayed to tea. She, Joan, was allowed butter with her bread and jam. That was only on great occasions. After that the Mothers' Union started. Mrs Haye must have stamped on the gossip, for all the women began coming again, every month. Mrs Haye attended herself the first time. Mother put some cut flowers in a pot just by her. It was a special occasion, so Father's objection to cutting flowers was forgotten. "Do you want the best rose tree to be the rubbish heap?" Later, there was a woman who tried to teach them how to make baskets, but she forgot how to make them herself in the middle, and nobody minded, they had gone on whispering just the same. They were great times, those.

A fat drop of rain plunked on to the window-sill. Rain. Then another, and another. The air became full of messages, a branch just underneath moved uneasily. There was a rumble miles away that trundled along the sky till it roared by overhead and burst in the distance. Thunder. Rain fell quicker. A broad flame of lightning – waiting, waiting for the crash. Ah. The storm was some way off. The rain walked up the scales of sound, swishing like a scythe swishes. Quick light from another flash lit up the yard, and a bird was flying as if pursued, across the snouted pump. Darkness. The thunder. Nearer.

The air was cool, unloaded. Joan drew back from the window, for she was being splashed by the spray as the drops smashed. The rain fell faster, faster. A terrific sheet of light and all the sky seemed to be tumbling down, moving celestial furniture. Father's bass came up singing confidently, "There is a green land far away." Daylight, the sky fought. Darkness and rain. Sheet lightning never hurt anything, but how wonderful to be as afraid as this. Father was rising on the tide of knowledge, "I know, I know," he cried, and heaven saluted it with her trumpets. He sang a line of the "Red Flag," but switched off. Swish, swish, said the rain, settling down to steadiness. Father was singing something and taking all the parts. The chickens in the hut made plaintive noises, the cock was being so tiresome. "What a bore the old man is," they were saying, "but we are so frightened of him." How wonderful, terror. Joan quaked on the box. Swish, said the rain.

Joan draws her blouse round her and hunches her shoulders. How much fresher it is now. The storm thunders away behind, it has passed over. Mumbles come from below. Laughter. All of her listens. His voice, "Ring out, wild bells." Always the church bells that he could not escape. Hunted by bells. Crash – the empty bottle. Then he is singing again. Mother had used to play. He is coming upstairs, toiling up, and Joan shivers. Into his room. Silence. Quietly he goes to bed and is asleep. The light in him had gone out. He had forgotten.

She feels cheated. He had been so mad underneath. Why hadn't he battered at the door? What a shame. All that trembling for nothing. He had forgotten her. She shuts the window and, lighting a candle, undresses and lets down her hair. She gets into bed. Sleep.

Eyes closed.

Sleep. Now she would go to sleep.

Turns over.

Sleep.

The lawn. The roses.

It can't have been sheet lightning because there was thunder. Then it had been dangerous.

A stands for ant. B stands for bee. C stands for cat. Sitting on Mother's knee tracing the tummy of a, her hand guiding.

Later on Mother tried to teach her other things. It used to be a great game to get as many "I don't know myself, dear's," out of her as possible in the morning.

There was the Vicarage pew every Sunday, Mrs Haye to the left, crazy Kate just behind, then the churchwarden, sniffling, sniffling, and two or three almshouse people. Father always preached out of the green book on the second shelf in the old study, though sometimes he talked about politics. Mrs Haye would stir violently when she disagreed, which would make Father stutter and Mother angry. Sometimes, though not very often, her son John would come too, he who was blind now. She used to watch him all through the service when he was there. He was so aloof, and there was nothing, no one else to look at. Nothing happened, no one did anything except the organist when she forgot. The service would go slowly on. Weston, the head gardener at Barwood, the only person in the choir, would sing as if he did not care. Father's voice toiled through the service. Mrs Haye argued the responses. The organist was paid to come, Weston only came that Mrs Haye might see that he came. Outside, through the little plain glass window at the side of their pew, the top of an apple tree waved. In summer there were apples on it which she used to pick in her imagination, and any time a bird might fly across, free. The service would go on and finish quite suddenly with a hymn, and then the run home with the blue hills in the distance, with the glimpse, just before the second gate, of the tower of the Abbey church, the greeting of Mrs Green who was always at her door at the beginning of the last field – no, the last but one, there was the orchard; dinner. It had all gone. Why, since she loved it so? The summers were so wonderful, the winter nights so comfortable. Gone. To-day had ended wrong and had started wrong. Forget in sleep.

The bed was too hot, the sheets clung, one leg was hot against the other. Her hair laid hot fingers about her face.

She pulled aside the bed-clothes and lay on top of them on her back, a white smudge in the dark. Outside tepid rain poured. This was cooler.

There was the clock that used to strike bed-time, half-past six. Had she heard the one stroke? Had she forgotten? But no.

"Bed-time, Joan."

"No, I don't want to."

"Now be a good girl."

To gain time – "Where's Daddy?"

"Now, Joan, you know your Daddy works all the evenings. Now go to bed, dearie. I'll come up and see you."

Starting in on the gin more likely. Oh, everything was very proper then. Where had he put the empties, though? Of course he can't have been bad as far back as that, it was only much later. Just before the Mothers' Meeting she had found Mrs Baxter sniffing round Father's room. She herself had smelt the smell too. She had called Mother, who had not noticed anything, of course. After that Father had said that he would dust the room himself, as he could not have his papers being fidgeted with.

"Fidget, fidget, that's all a woman is when cleaning. Tidying up means hiding. There is an order in my disorder. Yesterday I spent half an hour looking for the church accounts which I found eventually, tidied away into the private correspondence. I can't bear it. You do understand, don't you, Mrs Baxter? Of course I am not blaming you in the least, but . . ."

"Very well, Mr Entwhistle. I understand, sir." Sniff!

Something like that, but it was the sniff. It was the first sign of a mystery that had been so exciting till she had known.

His private correspondence. That can't have been anything. Only letters to Mrs Haye – oh, yes, and to the Bishop. He had scored off the Bishop one day. A great thing. Butter with her bread and jam that day.

But times had been hard. Really they were better off here. The food had dwindled, she had felt hungry a good deal.

"A wage less than a labourer."

"Oh, yes."

"What's that? Well, isn't it?"

"It wouldn't be."

"Well then, approximately. And then there are your clothes to buy and the child's."

"And your personal expenses. What you waste."

"What? I suppose I can't spend a penny on myself?"

"Run along, Joan, and play."

"Yes, Mummy."

Then Uncle Jim, whose death they had waited for so long, died in France. Of fever or something. He had no child and had left all his money to "the poor fellow he's a parson." Lord, that joke. Father had seen it in the *Evangelical Supplement* and had used it for ever when he talked. However, things had become a bit easier then, and probably the spirit merchant had begun to give tick again.

Only one villager had been killed.

"And I said to them, I put it to them point-blank, 'I won't sign the minutes when no member of the Parochial Council comes to church,' I said."

What was there to get for to-morrow? Milk, more sardines, and some more candles. Perhaps that book Mrs Donner had in her window for thruppence. She could put the thruppence down to the bread. The title was so thrilling, *The Red Love of White Hope, Scioux, Matt.*

She had not read many books in the old days. There was the *Water Babies*, and one or two others, but she had forgotten. And *Robinson Crusoe*. After that she hadn't read at all. She didn't really know what she had done. She had sat on the wall a good deal, asking why and how the world was here, and watching people go by. Silly to trouble about why the world was – it was, that was all. On Saturdays in summer dusty motor cars would clatter by on the way to the riverside pub. Birmingham people they were. There were other people sometimes. And four times a day the milk lorry came by with him driving it. Fascinating he was, he looked so wicked.

Was Scioux the name of a town, or did it mean that White Hope was a Red Indian? Mrs Donner might let her have a look inside. If it was only a town she would not buy it, but with a Red Indian it should be meaty. Then, again, she used to go up to watch the village blacksmith shoe the horses or repair a plough, and he would let her work the handle of the bellows and make the sparks spray out. The corners of his forge had been wonderful, all sorts of odds and ends of rusty iron, and always the chance, as he said, of finding something very valuable among them. Little innocent. But above all there was the blacksmith himself. He was very stupid but the strongest man that ever lived. It was wonderful, his strength. She had tried to lift the big hammer one day, and she had let it drop on her big toe, it was so heavy. Wouldn't be able to lift it now, even. He had had to carry her back to the Vicarage. Mother had been very angry. But then the days were gone when she kissed to make it well. Poor right big toe.

Occasionally they had gone into Norbury. There used to be the old horse bus along the main road to take you in, and then you were in the middle of the hum and bustle of it, hundreds of people hurrying along in town clothes. Norbury was wonderful with its three thousand inhabitants. And there was Green the draper's, Mother fingering the stuffs for her new dress – would it wash, would it wear? it did not look to her like very good quality. And the boot shop, Dapp's, with the smell of leather and hundreds and hundreds of shoes hung about, and the shop assistant's hair – like a cascade of glue, Father said once outside, but it wasn't, it smelt lovely – and his way of tying the shoe on, that little finger. Fool. He would be married now, and she, whoever she was, would have someone to wait for in the evenings, to kiss or to have rows with, and wear his ring. She would have his children, and they would watch them together. And the farmers, fat and thin, in their pony carts, getting down at the Naiad's Calf to have a drink. Father had hated the farmers; "they are making a lot of money," was what he said. And as evening came on they went sometimes to tea at the Deanery, and she would doze by the fire, sitting very correctly in her chair, hearing the boom of the Dean's voice to Father, and Mother's shrill complaint to the Dean's wife, dozing after the huge tea that she had eaten when they weren't looking. They would have a fit if she went there now.

She hadn't been in Norbury for ages. There was Mrs Donner who sold everything. She was a one, that woman. Three and six for a bit of stuff which she wouldn't like to put on a horse's back to keep the cold off!

It had been hard work following Mother about. She had hurried so from shop to shop. She must have been hungry for town life again. Those that are townbred hate the country. They used always to eat lunch in the Cathedral Tea Rooms. Mrs Oliver, big and fat, who looked after the customers, always came up and said, "Ah, Mr Entwhistle, so you've come to see us townsfolk again, sir." Mother would bring out the sandwiches. After they had eaten Mother and she would go off to the shops again, while Father went back to the Library. Mother used to call Mrs Oliver "a designing woman" – sour grapes. And the chemist, mysterious behind his spectacles, in his shop made of shelves and bottles, and cunningly-piled cardboard boxes. The jolting ride home in the dark, with the walk at the end.

Then there was Nancy. All the last years at the Vicarage had been Nancy. What had become of her now? Married with children, most likely, but not to the baker's son she had been so gone on. Nancy, with her fairest hair and skinny legs, she was not nearly as good-looking as her. Her snub nose, and the small watery pink eyes.

They had met in a lane, had smiled, and had made friends. That is, they had never really made friends, she had been far too stupid. But Nancy used to giggle at her jokes, and she liked that. Dolly had been forgotten then.

They talked a great deal about men, with long silences, and Nancy's giggle and "Oh you's." They walked arm in arm, or more often with their arms round each other's waists, their heads bent, whispering. Lord, what fools they must have looked. Of course Mother was only too glad that she was out of the way, Father too.

They used to walk most in the lane, just outside the house here. She had been in love, oh, how passionate, with Jim who never spoke, and who worked for Mr Curry. He had been worse than George. But he used sometimes to come home by the lane in the evening, and they would pass him arm in arm. She would give him the sidelong look she had practised in the mirror, but he never did more than touch his cap. She had dropped her handkerchief once, as Nancy had told her they did in the world. They had talked and giggled for days before she had plucked up courage to do it. But of course he did nothing.

Nancy wore a ring round her neck on a bit of cotton. She said at first that Alfred had given it her, but that time under the honeysuckle when she had shown Nancy her birthmark on her leg, she had confessed that she had only got it out of a cracker at Christmas. Nancy used to think her awfully daring.

Then their walks when evening was coming on, when they wandered down the sunken lane. Thick sunlight and thicker shade, when they twined closer together, and walked slower, and were silent. There was the heavy smell of honeysuckle, sweet, which a little fresh air coming down between the banks would begin to blow away. The birds flew quietly from side to side, there were flowers whose names she did not know, and long tufts of grass full of dew. The flowers made dots of colour in the shade, the ground they walked on buried the sound of their feet . . . Soon they would come to the gate, and they would sit clinging to each other and balancing, watching the horses scrunch up the grass and the cows lie chewing, idly content. The sky was always different, and the end of a hot day was sleepy. The flies buzzed round, the midges bit. On a piece of fresh manure there would be hundreds of brown flies, and a bee would hurry by. She used to watch the trees most often. There were so many of them, one behind the other, hiding, showing, huddled, alone. Far away a car would blow a horn, or a train would whistle, but it used to feel as if there was everything between them and it. Birds up in the sky that was paling would fly silently with a purpose. They were going to bed, and soon she would go back, have supper, and go to bed. Partridges talked to each other anxiously, as they gathered together, against the dangers of the night. The horses looked round calmly. A dog barked miles away.

Then, as it was getting dark, they would part to go home. Nancy up to the village, and she herself across the fields to the Vicarage. The cows would not rise, and the horses would give her barely a glance. Only a rabbit perhaps would sit up, drum the ground, and flee to his burrow. And he would not bother to go down it, for as soon as she had passed he would be back again nibbling. In spring there would be lambs, absurd and delicious on their long·weak legs.

She would climb a warm gate and feel the wet of the dew soaking through her stockings. In front was the Vicarage, all the windows open, waiting, and her glass of milk and biscuits. She would climb the last gate and cross the dusty road, lift the latch of the door in the wall, and the roses, the white ones and the red ones, would greet her. Father might be sitting in the deck-chair on the lawn, smoking his pipe, the blue smoke going lazily up to the other blue of the sky. Mother might be sewing just inside the French window. The milk was cool.

And then she would go up the stairs into her room, the little white bed, the texts round the walls, the open window letting in the dim light and the roses. And she would go to sleep and – was she going to cry?

All gone, the lawn, the roses, the quiet, the protection, her little room, the glass of milk, Jack, the horses, the cows, the walks, for they were not the same, Nancy, those evenings. Fool. The peace, the untroubledness, the old wall, the . . . All . . .

She went to sleep.

"My dear B. G.

"I saw you last night in the club, but you cut me dead. Come to lunch Friday to be forgiven. I wanted to talk about poor John. I am so sorry about it. Poor dear, amusing John. I must write to him, though what there is to say I don't know. Really, these letters of condolence are very difficult.

"But why did you cut me like that? I saw David Plimmer the other night and he spoke of you with enthusiasm. Don't forget about lunch Friday, if you cut that I shall know the worst.

"Yrs.———

"Seymour."

Part Three

BUTTERFLY

CHAPTER I

Waiting

He was in the summer-house. Light rain crackled as it fell on the wooden roof, and winds swept up, one after the other, to rustle the trees. A pigeon hurried rather through his phrase that was no longer now a call. Cries of rooks came down to him from where they would be floating, whirling in the air like dead leaves, over the lawn. The winds kept coming back, growing out of each other, and when a stronger one had gone by there would be left cool eddies slipping by his cheek, while a tree further on would thunder softly. Every wind was different, and as he listened to their coming and to their going, there was rhythm in their play. In the fields, beyond where the trees would be, a man cracked his whip, and a cow lowed. The long grass copied the trees with a tiny dry rustling.

But there was something new to-day; he had met her; he would meet her again, and the wind was lighter for it, the branches danced almost. He had been shy when they had met, and so had she, and he had laughed at himself for being shy, though that was all part of the game. For now at last he could play as the trees were doing now, advance, retreat, and it was a holiday, and she would be wild, so wild. Mamma was horrified at her life, she must have had a queer time, so that she would be interesting. And her voice had been afraid; she had been frightened at his lack of eyes. She would be fascinated later, as he lay by her side – oh, devilry – to listen to her hoarse voice, to weave question and answer.

There had been doubt in Mamma's voice when speaking

about her, and it had only been through pity that she had brought her to the house. He was old enough to know now, she had said, that the girl lived a most extraordinary life with her drunken father, that she was not quite proper. As if he had not always known, as if he had not told at once from her voice. But she, Mamma, had met her in the lane, looking so ill, with her hand all swollen and the thumb tied up in a rag, a rag-an'-bone man's rag, and she, Mamma, had said to herself that after all the girl was a parishioner, and she had positively insisted on her coming back to the house at once, that the thumb might be properly done up. And at first the girl had been sulky and silent, and then the poor girl had become quite servile in her thanks. That dreadful man, her father.

So they had met. But Mamma's voice had been uneasy all through her account of it; she had been frightened. She had told him that artists married barmaids continually and were unhappy ever after. And he had said that unhappiness was necessary to artists, and she had called that stuff and nonsense. But they had met. For Mamma had feared before he had gone blind that he would marry beneath him – well, not quite that, but someone unsuitable; and just lately she had been talking a great deal about marriage, how he must marry, how he must make a home for himself here. Her voice had been full of plans.

Voices had become his great interest, voices that surrounded him, that came and went, that slipped from tone to tone, that hid to give away in hiding. There had been wonder in hers when he had groped into the room upon them both; she had said, "Look." But before she had opened her mouth he had known that there was someone new in the room.

Voices had been thickly round him for the past month, all kinds of them. Mamma extracted them from the neighbourhood, and all had sent out the first note of horror, and some had continued horrified and frightened, while others had grown sympathetic, and these were for the most part the fat voices of mothers, and some had been disgusted. She had been the first to be almost immediately at her ease, when she spoke it was with an eager note, and there were so few eager people.

To-morrow June (her name was June) would come to have her poor hand attended to. She had cut it, and it was poisoned a little, poor little hand. "Like white mice," her fingers. They would not be white though, but hard and a little dirty with work. To-morrow.

To-day Mamma had gone into Norbury in one of her fits of righteous anger. On the road and in front of the town rubbish heap, just where you had the best view of the Abbey, the Town Council had allowed a local man to build a garage, in tin, painted red. Of course, she had said, there was jobbery in it, and there probably was. So she had gone to the Dean, and she would be talking to him now. The Dean would boom sympathy, and he would be tired, poor man, but he would write to the Town Council. They would do nothing. Poor Ruskin!

Still it was a pity, for the garage spoilt that view. But they had not tampered with the inside of the church. It was quiet in there as the country round, and all was simple, and the round pillars were so kind, and the echoes that blurred everything and so made the words more grand. The church music went round and round the walls, and then rolled along the ceiling till the shifting notes built walls about you till you were yourself very high up, so that you could see.

But Mamma always made one go to Barwood Church, where the service was out of tune and where there was not even simplicity, for Crayshaw lit candles and wore vestments. And outside always there were quiet fields and colour to show you how absurd it was to worship indoors. Crayshaw had just had another baby, a son, and he had so many. But Mamma said that they must go to Barwood

127

Church that they might be an example to the village. So they went, and the few others they met there went to show that they went, and everyone realised that, and so on.

Last Sunday, the first time he had been after going blind, there had been voices singing in the county accent. Such nice, strong, genuine voices. But then Crayshaw had spoilt it all by preaching about blindness in the East, ophthalmia in the Bible, spittle and sight, with a final outburst against pagans. During the sermon he had fingered his prayer-book; it was longer and thinner than any of the rest. It had been presented for his first service in church. And he should have been sentimental over it; he should have thought how good he had been so long ago in the nursery, of how he had wanted to be a bishop, and of how Mabel Palmer had said how nice it would be for the neighbourhood to own a bishop.

Things were different now. The nursery was gone and the days at Noat, so full of people, were gone. There were other things instead. There was so much to find out, and, in a sense, so much to discover for others, for when one was blind one understood differently. A whole set of new values had arisen. And being blind did not hurt so long as one did not try to see in terms of sight what one touched or heard.

The wind was higher and the summer-house groaned now and then in it. The trees roared, when suddenly there would be lulls, strangely quiet, waiting for another wind to come up. Everything would be stopped short. The branches were still, and would be looking vacantly at each other, like children come to the end of a game. Then a wind comes up and covers the emptiness that had followed; a dead branch snapped and fell to the ground. It was getting colder; the sun had not been out all day, and one always knew when the sun was out. A blackbird warned as he fled down wind. The air round was stealthy.

It was all so full of little hints; the air carried up little noises and then hurried them away again. The silence had been so full. The rain had stopped falling now, and he was straining to catch the slightest secrets that were in the winds, and before he had never known that. In a way one gained by being blind, of course one did; besides he was happy to-day, for was not she coming to-morrow?

So that they would go for walks together, and he would get her to lead him to the top of Swan's Wood to look upon the view there and listen to her eager voice. What a pity never to see that view again – the river, the meadows, the town, the rubbish heap, the Abbey and the hills behind. And the one hill, a mound, that came before the line of hills in the distance, and that had things dotted about on it, and through them a road, a quiet yellow line, which had clung to it and had shown off the hollows.

When they were there they would talk of everything, and he would find out her life, why her hand was like that, and why she trembled the air in a room. He would teach her the view, and she would be so bored with it as she would so want to go on talking about that. A wind would come down to wreathe rings about them – how lyrical! But June would be so charming; she must be, and she had such strong hands. Besides, her voice was lovely; there was something wild in it and something asleep there as well, as if she too had lived alone and had many things to tell. For she would be interesting at least; she must have suffered living in the cottage that was falling down now, and she would be able to tell of it, and she would have had some contact with horrible things so that she would not be vapid. So many of the young ladies he met were like Dresden china. And she would be . . . well, no; there was no word for it. But they would go on walking out together like any boy and his slut, and he would explore in her for the things that her voice told him were there, and that had never been let out. For no one saw her or would speak to her.

It was so necessary to talk; you had to, and with someone

who could understand or sympathise with your ideas. How they would talk, June and he, for she must and would understand how he needed someone young. When you were blind and beginning to make discoveries, you had to tell them to somebody; besides, talking was the only thing you could do as well as anyone else. And surely she would not dance, for who was there to dance with her, unless there was another man? Perhaps there was, and then the whole dull round of country conversation would go round again, and when one had gone through it so often before. Let them talk about things, not people. And then, of course, they could talk about themselves.

Why had he never learnt to play the piano? It would be so nice to be able to sit down and make the lazy notes ripple through this echoing house, up the stairs and through doors and windows to be lost in the wetness of the garden. She had known how. She had played music wandering out to the gossamer, and so quiet; as raindrops gather on a twig and then slip off, so had her notes fallen in such a silver, liquid sound. But then the sun came out. It was changed now. The hut, the trees and each leaf suddenly had a spirit of their own. And the wind bore them down to you that they might whisper in your ear, and be companions as you sat in the dark. So that you were not really lonely; there were only the deaf who were really cut off. How dreadful to be deaf, not to hear this wind choosing out the leaves and carrying them down gently that they might rustle on the ground.

Would June be like this? So that she could sit still and listen. Surely she would not want to break out into a great screaming laugh to announce that someone had been hurt, or something broken? She also might have dreams and be able to understand his, perhaps. And yet she would not be sickly, but rather like a sunflower, absorbing from the sun, and so proud, so still. Women were like flowers; it was silly, but they were. The sudden flutter of wings of a bird who was going elsewhere to drink more in and pour it out again to the sun brought the grass and trees together, and the earth that kept them both. Women understood like that. Their intuitions exalted them to the simple understanding of the trees, for trees were so simple; there was no remoteness in them as of mountains and their false sublimity. But he had not met any women who were women. Still, June felt like that, and her loneliness would have taught her silence, for she could not have met many people.

As long as she was not like Miss Blandair – but then how could she be? Miss Blandair, whom Mamma had had to stay, who played tennis so very well, who danced, and was so very suitable. She had been so bright as she cackled on, and Mamma had approved; her voice had been rotund with approval. She had made him very weary; hers was such wasted energy. What energy one had should be put away secretly for the thing in hand, not thrown to the wind in handfuls of confetti. For then one saw it in retrospect only, lying rather tarnished on the ground.

All June would be stored up.

But it was an anxious time for Mamma, waiting to see him settled. And it was the end, to settle down. He could not; one did not dare to. It was not fair to Mamma, but what could one do? She was not his mother; she had only made herself into one, though that was just the same. But he must go out with June; there was so much to talk about, so much sympathy to be sought after. For they were all so old, one could not talk to them; they did not understand, in spite of their always saying they did. Nurse had been young but too full of her trade.

And Nanny had not been so well lately. She had been more hesitating on the walks and her shoes had creaked more slowly. Mamma had said something about it, how Nanny must take care of herself, and she had given her some medicine. Nanny was talking more and more as time went on, that afternoon when he had been told she had talked far more than she would have done in the old days. She had a cough now that was becoming more and more frequent, a juicy cough, that seemed to tear her, and that was horrible to hear. Poor Nanny! For she was a link with so much that was gone; she had seen the house before he had come to it, or rather just after he had arrived. She had known those who lived in it, and she had known him so long that they were used to each other, so that they had a few worn jokes at which they laughed together, and that was all; there was really no conversation left, nor was it necessary. She had been so jealous of the nurse. The hours he had spent making it all right again!

She had known his mother, Mummy. She had a very few stories about her, such nice stories, and he would make her tell them again and again, when perhaps a new story would come out. Mummy must have been so charming, they had all loved her so.

She was like a dream, something so far away that came back sometimes. And now that he was blind he had come to treasure little personal things of her own, a prayer-book of hers, though that, of course, was mistaken; a pair of kid gloves, so soft to touch, and they had a faint suggestion of her about them, so faint, that gently surrounded them and made them still more soft. And she had died because of him.

There was so little that he knew about her, only what Nanny could tell. He never saw anyone who had known her, and Mamma was always trying, ever since she had told him by letter how he was not her son, to put herself in Mummy's place. How silly to go on calling her by that name; she had been dead nearly nineteen years now; it was so sentimental. But the word was fresh, it clung about the gloves. They had been cold so long, those gloves.

From what Nanny said she had been so happy in the house, going about lightly from place to place. One really did not know anything about her; Nanny had only seen her once and her stories were only what the other servants had told her. They would have been seated round in the kitchen waiting for the funeral, and they would have talked and talked, weeping in turns, and Nanny had learnt what she knew in that way. There were none of them left; he had never known them, for Mamma had sent them all away when she had married Father and gone to India. But apparently she had whistled most beautifully; Nanny's descriptions never went beyond "beautiful," and he could hear her going about whistling gently till the house was full of shadows. She must have linked everything up with it. And then apparently she had played the piano quite beautifully.

Such ages ago he had been at Noat, only a few months, but still – the misery of those days, their dreariness, and with their strange exaltations now and then. So much depended on whether people were nice to you or not. And the Art Society with the marionette shows. There had been no one at J. W. P.'s to mind about such things. It was getting cold out here. Heat drew one out, one was with a companion. Just as their glow against each other would draw them out – June and he.

Mummy would have helped, then and now. She would have had such a gentle understanding, so that when he came back from Noat for the holidays they would have sat by the fire and talked it out. What evenings, and what quiet grey days with the colours in the fields washed into luminous clarity, and the calm in the trees. She would have understood all that with her tender whistling, and they would have walked, perhaps, silently happy together to the top of Swan's Wood. Or down to the river with its surprises and the quietly-flowing water.

For she would have seen things by the light of intuitions, often wrong, but no less enchanting, and by discovering things in other people she would have shown herself. How silly people were to think a grey day sad; it was really so full of happiness, while the sun only made things reflect the sun, and so not be themselves. Dew came in the morning with the light sky above and sent pearl colours over the fields, and so made him think of her, who was so like that herself.

There were so many things to do, all the senses to develop, old acquaintances of childhood to make friends with again. To sit still and be stifled by the blackness was wrong; he had done that long enough. The temptation was so great, the darkness pressed so close, and what sounds one heard could only at first be converted into terms of sight and not of sound. When a blackbird fled screaming he had only been able to see it as a smudge darting along, and he had tried in vain to visualise it exactly. Now he was beginning to see it as a signal to the other birds that something was not right; it was the feeling that one has in the dark when something moves, and when one jumps to turn on the light, and the light leaps out through the night. Why translate into terms of seeing, for perhaps he would never see again, even in his dreams? They might be of sounds or of touch now. The deaf might dream of a soundless world, and how cold that would be. There was the story of the deaf old man who had forgotten that the breaking waves of the sea on the beach made sound. He must not go deaf; one clung so to what senses were left. But sight was not really necessary; the values of everything changed, that was all. There was so much in the wind, in the feel of the air, in the sounds that Nature lent one for a little, only to take away again. Or was there nothing in all these? Why did everyone and everything have to live on illusion, that Mummy was really near, and as the meaning of everything? But one could not let that go.

June was an illusion – a lovely one. He had never felt anyone so alive. Coming into that room had been like a shower of sparks, or was it merely the mood he had been in? There were days when everything bristled with life, the mahogany table in the front hall almost purred when you stroked it, it was so warm and clinging. Great feline table. And the flowers poked their soft heads so confidingly into your palm, tickling. They must get another dog now that Ruffles was dead that he might have his hands licked. Stroking June, her skin would be so alive. There were days when everything was a toy, and when even the big flowers with heavy scents condescended, except the wooden lilies, and they stank of pollution. Violets were silly; they were not bold enough; they nestled simpering and were too frightened. But the others would play with you if you would only let them, gay exquisite things.

He would write about these things, for life was only beginning again, and there were many things to say. Besides, one couldn't for ever be sitting in a chair like this, and be for the rest of one's life someone to be sorry for. And perhaps the way he saw everything was the right way, though there could be no right way but one's own. Art was what was created in the looker-on, and he would have to try and create in others. He would write slowly, slowly, and his story would drift as the country drifted, and it would be about trivial things. The man who chased tulips on a bicycle was silly as well as being an idiot, but the piano-tuner might make a story. He was of the type that had to feel over your face before he became confidential. Why hadn't he done that to Miss Blandair? Of all practices it was the most revolting, and far more for yourself. Faces were so deformed, your fingers strayed into hair suddenly, though shut eyelids were incredibly alive. Not that the piano-tuner ever became confidential. He was very unhappy and very secretive. He had been blinded in the war, and the injustice of it made his hands burn when he talked about it. He gave himself away so painfully when he played after the tuning was over. But he had a few interesting things to say, how you would find when you were blind a little longer that you could tell by a feeling in your face when a wall or a chair or even something so low as a footstool was coming.

So that you could walk about alone and unaided as he did. It would be wonderful, this new sense, he looked forward to it so, and was often imagining objects in the way when there were none. It would give a new feeling of companionship with the world. The darkness would be more intimate.

But it would all be so different with her about. So that they would all go for walks together, all of them. There would be Mummy to take up to the top of Swan's Wood, and of course June to take there, too, and Nanny to go round the garden on his arm, and Mamma to accompany visiting in the village. What talks they would have, telling Mummy what June was like, Nanny how inferior June was, and Mamma how sorry he was for June, though she would see through that. So that this, perhaps, was a beginning with June and the birds and the trees. They were much nearer, and Mummy was, too. The days would have change in them now.

It was charming to think of Mummy being so close, but she wasn't. And June was so much more tangible. It was also charming to think of the trees as being in conspiracy with the birds to make life more endurable, but of course they weren't. One lived, that was all, and at times one lived more than at other times. But they were charming illusions, and they became real if you believed them. Oh! why did he think these things?

Those gloves and things of hers, why did they have so much of her about them? And why did the trees and the birds conspire together so openly? And why when he was alone did some presence – some companion of days that were dead now, because he could not remember them – why did she come and walk with him and sit by his side and make him understand dimly through his blindness? Mamma would come upon them when they were alone together sometimes, and she would say that he must not become morbid. And she would talk and talk until the longing went away.

Was that what it was – a longing? Would he come upon it suddenly?

There was no pain in his memory of her; if there had been it would have driven her away. That was why it was so lucky he had never known her; another illusion would have gone. Why did he go on thinking these things? Then it was lucky perhaps that he could not see any more, that the little boy had taken his sight away. For she was nearer than she had ever been before, now that he was blind.

Evening was coming and with it the soft, harping rain, rustling, rustling. A bird was muttering liquidly, gently somewhere, and it was very like the night – kind, strange. And she was here with the feel of the air, and June was to-morrow, tangible as the sunlight. He shivered, and getting up he went into the house.

CHAPTER II

Walking Out

"My name isn't June, it's Joan, and always was."

"But do you mind my calling you June? I think June is such a lovely name, so much nicer than Joan. You are just like June, too."

"Why should I be like June? You are silly. But I don't mind. You can have your own way if you like, though I don't know why you shouldn't like Joan, which is my name whether you like it or not."

"That is the only reason why I like it."

"You are clever."

"But when June is your name I like it better than all other names, don't you?"

"No, I don't."

"Oh, well, I will call you Joan, if June is not to your fancy."

"No, have it your own way."

"That is most awfully nice of you. I . . . No."

It was not going too well. It was so hard to find anything to talk about, and she was not easy. There was a terribly strained feeling in the air, they were feeding on each other's shyness. But it would be better next time. The ice must break.

"Where are we now?"

"We're just coming to the stile into Mr Cume's orchard."

"Then it was here that the bulldog attacked a cow. Most alarming it was. Flew at her nose."

"No, he didn't, did he?"

"Yes, but I pulled him off. Do you like bulldogs?"

"I don't know, I haven't seen very many. I only saw yours once or twice, and then he rather frightened me."

"He was so tame, really."

There was a pause. They walked on.

"Do you like dogs?"

"I don't know. No."

"You don't like dogs! Oh, June, I love them."

"I like cats."

"No, I don't like cats. They are so funny and mysterious, or is that just what you like about them?"

"Father doesn't like cats either."

"Doesn't he?"

"No, he doesn't!"

"Have you got a cat?"

"Yes, he's called Minnie."

"They are so nice to have about the house – pets, I mean."

"Yes, aren't they?"

A pause. She was wonderful, so shy and retiring. What was there to say? He sought for words.

"Will you come for another walk with me one day?"

"Perhaps."

"We could go to the top of Swan's Wood. It would be very nice of you. I am so alone."

"Why do you want to go up to the top? What happens there?"

– What would? "There is a view, that's all. A lovely view that I used to look at a great deal in the old days. And you can describe it to me when we get there."

"All right. Though I don't know what you see in views."

He was a queer person, but very exciting.

They walked. He guided his steps from the sound of hers. He felt awkward. Then he stumbled and almost fell, on purpose. She stopped and laid a hand on his arm.

"Take care. You mustn't fall down and hurt yourself."

"There is no harm done. I say, June, would you mind

dreadfully if I did put my hand on your arm? I should be able to get along easier then."

"If you want to."

They set out again. Was it imagination or did she press his arm under hers, close to her? Had she much on? His heart beat, one felt that one could never say anything again. Wasn't she wonderful!

"Do you like cows?"

"I don't know. Why?"

"They frighten me sometimes, although I live most of the time in the country. Don't they you?"

"No, I don't think so."

"But they looked so fierce with their horns, and sometimes when they were frightened in Norbury market their eyes went purple and they slavered at the mouth."

"They are very stupid, that's all."

"I'm not sure. And bulls, of course, are really dangerous."

"Bulls?" She laughed.

"I like calves, June."

"Yes, calves are all right. They are so funny when they are young an' their legs go wobbly."

He laughed. That was a little more human of her.

"But they are awfully dangerous when they are like that, for the mother is only too ready to attack you, isn't she?"

"Quite likely. Don't men fight bulls in Spain or some place like that?"

"Yes, they do. And in England they used to set bulldogs on to bulls, so it's in their blood. That was why ours went for Crayshaw's cow. But I should have thought that they ought to stage cat-and-dog fights."

"Oh?"

Back to cats again. But his arm was in hers, and it was warm there.

"There's a gate coming."

"The one into the road?"

"Yes, that's it. Mind, you mustn't hurt yourself."

She guided him through, and his feet felt the stones.

"Well, this is where I leave you. I'll walk back by the road."

"Will you be all right?"

"Yes. You will be coming to-morrow to have your hand looked to, won't you?"

"I expect so."

"Poor hand, I am so sorry about it. Does it hurt very much?"

"It does rather."

Here was someone to make a fuss over it, and it did hurt too.

"I'm so sorry."

There was a pause. They faced each other in the middle of the road. His head was on one side and he didn't seem to know where she was quite. Poor blind young man, she was sorry for him. He must be looked after.

The awkwardness had fallen again between them. There was nothing to say. But she had agreed to come up to Swan's Wood, which was one good thing. She was very nice.

"Well, perhaps I had better be going back."

"Yes, an' so had I."

"Good-bye."

"Good-bye."

And he began to walk home. Their first meeting was over. It had been terrifying. But they had walked arm in arm anyway. The touch and the warmth were so much finer when one was blind. And one was more frightened; still, her voice had been kind. She would come again right enough. He touched his blue glasses, he must be a sight. His steps sounded hollowly on the road, and he thought of a dream when he had run and run and run. But there had been no birds then, they had all been hushed. For suddenly the sun came out, and, warmed by him, a bird began to sing in little cascades of friendliness. How good the world was. He wanted his lunch.

★ ★ ★

Nanny sat by the fire. Shadows ran up and down the walls of her room, and it was very quiet in there except for her breathing and the murmuring kettle. Kettles were so companionable. On the table by her side was a cup of tea which steamed up at the ceiling, broadly at first, and then the steam narrowed down till at last it was lost in a pin-prick. It could not get so high. On the table was a patchwork cover, the heirloom of her family. By the cup stood a tea-caddy and by that a spoon. The kettle spurted steam at the fender in sudden, angry bursts.

It was close in her room because she never opened the window. Her black dress rose stiffly up against the heat, and the whalebone in her collar kept the chin from drooping. Little flames would come up to lick the kettle, and then the shadows on the wall would jump out of the room. But she sat straight and quiet as the people in the photographs round. She was of their time. Only her breathing, tired and hoarse, helped the kettle to break the quiet of the watching photographs.

It wasn't right his going out with her like this. This would be the third time he had gone out with her, and it wasn't like Mrs Haye to allow it it ought to be stopped. At that age they could so easily fall in love with each other. And what would happen then? Young people always went into those things blind, they didn't see what the consequences of their actions were. He ought to be more careful of whom he took up with. *His* daughter, indeed. What would everyone be saying? And that *her* boy should go out with that thing, him that she had brought up since he was a squalling babby, it was not right.

There had been the time when he had first been given to

142

her – a wonderful baby strong as you could wish, full seven and a half pounds from the moment he was born, and since then she had fed him with her own hands just like as she was doing now, and getting up at nights constant when he was hollering for his pap. She had seen him grow up right from the beginning. And he had gone blind – it couldn't have been worse! – so that now he could never have a good time with the young ladies or nothing, poor Master Johnnie! But she would see him out of this thing that had come upon them, she had seen him out of many such – there had been the time when he had been taken with whooping cough a deal of trouble they had had with him, but they had pulled him through. Mrs Haye had been such a good mother to him better indeed than his real one Mrs Richard Haye would ever have been. There were stories the servants that were with her told but then, what was the good of believing stories but from what was said she was too free altogether. You can never trust men not even your husband's best friend but there it was!

And Master John had growed up and gone to college but that never had agreed with him, he was weakly ever since she could remember. It was what she said that had kept him from a preparatory school even if the doctor had said so too. Then they had had the governess who was not up to much with all her airs and graces. The way she used to carry on with that teacher in Norbury, undignifying. But he had been too weakly for college, he had never been happy there even if he had growed to the figure of a man he was. The other boys what were less well-behaved and brought up would have always been at him, she knew their ways. And there had come a time when he would hardly so much as throw a glance at her and say "Hullo, Nanny," and Mr William had said one day "He is growing up," and she had seen him going away from her when the only things she could do for him was to darn his socks and sew on buttons, but he was back to her now, she could help him again bring him up his food and take him out for walks. It wasn't right that hussy taking hold on him and everyone would be talking you see if they didn't.

Then the master had married again and a good thing too for the first one wasn't such as to waste breath over. Beautiful she had been, too beautiful they was a danger them lovely ones though what he could see in this hussy she didn't know but then he couldn't see, poor Master John that was what it was. There had been great goings on for the marriage, a servants' ball and the service in church had been lovely the bridesmaids being in pink and the clergyman having a lovely voice. She had been a good mistress to her Mrs Haye had been, only a hard word now and then from that day on. And she had made a good mother to Master John, always thinking of him and looking after him just as if he was her own boy. Then the master going to India with his regiment and leaving her with Master John to live with the grandparents, what was dead now some time, and where they didn't treat her proper they was half-starving the poor boy. They hadn't no illusions of his mother but it wasn't his fault poor little mite what she was. And then their coming back after she had wrote to tell them, though the regiment did come back too, and his falling downstairs dead as mutton his heart having gone sudden like. A lovely funeral it was and a fine corpse he made lying out on the bed. In the church it was the men of the estate that carried the coffin, and the church was draped in black, and there were officers from the regiment and wreaths that the officers had sent and some from the men. Everything had been done in style. And the mistress had been splendid. Quite soon after she had said to her "Well Jennings it is up to us to bring him up" and she had said back "We will'm."

And then he had begun to crawl round the nursery, very fond of coal he had been, and always full of mischief. And they had all said then what a fine man he was going to grow up into, and so he is, but they none of them had the gift of sight so they couldn't have foretold this. When she had been told she was sitting in this chair as like as she might be now and she said "Lord have mercy on us" she remembered it as if it was yesterday, though it did seem an age away, and that only six months really. In the next room in the old day-nursery was all the toys he used to have and her first thought was that he would never be able to play with them again. You got a bit mixed up with time when you grew older. They were all in the cupboard there the tin soldiers scarlet and blue with some cannon and the spotted horse which he used to be that fond of and the marbles with colours inside that he always wanted to swallow, they was a peril them things, and the box of bricks as he grew older so that they said he was going to be an architeck, and what would he be now? He had loved his toys, she could remember his sitting on his heels and getting excited over the soldiers as if they was real and fighting a real battle. They were all there in the cupboard waiting. Nothing had been lost and now that her time was coming perhaps when she was gone they would throw them away or give them away or give them to some poor child instead of keeping them, maybe for his children if he had any. Waste that was.

Would he marry now? And would a young lady want to marry a blind young man? Ah, but if they knew her Master John of course they would. She ought to know him, she had known him longer than anyone now, and he was so good and kind-hearted even if he was a bit rough at times, but then all young people were like that. She would like to see his son but she might go off at any minute, the doctor said so, it was her heart, she wouldn't last on to see him. But it wasn't doing him no good to be following around of that girl with her father. That man, and him in the church too, it was a sacrilege that's what it was. And the shame on the village and on the house. They was the laughing-stock of the countryside. And him going and living quite near just to spite them, oh if the master was here, he would send him packing and that daughter of his parading of herself about. She would talk to Mrs Haye she ought to know what everyone was saying.

She had been sitting in this very chair when who should come in but Mr William and she could see something was up on account of his being out of breath and he had said "The young master'as been 'urt" he said, and she had been turned to stone so to speak, as it says in the Book, and he had gone on about the accident on the railway and how he would be blind for ever. And she had said "Lord have mercy on us. Lord have mercy on us."

To think that it should happen to him, him that was so good and kind. He had been good to her he knew what he had to thank her for. And he had been so brave through it all. Oh dear. Even when he was quite a mite he had been that kind-hearted. Mrs Richard Haye was like that they had said. In another way though it must have been. And she always going about whistling, never going to church, and so happy with all her men friends hanging around and the master too simple to notice or suspect. Folks as are that happy are dangerous. And her silly whistling so that you couldn't stir without hearing it, senseless it was. And everything in such a muddle so they said. She had only seen her once when they had taken her to be shown to the mistress as the new nurse. Too weak she had been to stir a finger but beautiful although so pale lying there on the bed propped up on cushions, the light shining on her face, blue eyes half-closed with long lashes and so thin with her last homecoming. She hadn't said a word just looked at her, they were beautiful eyes, too beautiful. But they was all liable to die like that all women. She had been near to marrying Joe Hawkins before she went out into service. She didn't regret it, she would do it again if she had the chance, though two Master Johnies didn't come but once in a lifetime.

Getting up with difficulty she made herself some fresh tea, hanging up the kettle-holder on a brass-headed nail that goggled like a golden eye from the wall. The room was thick with warmth. A lifeless pennant of steam came from the spout of the teapot.

She lifted the cup to her lips with hands which trembled rather. She sipped. A cup o' tea did you a deal of good. Nothing like it so that the older you were the more you felt the need of it. And the cough was getting worse, it wouldn't go till it had killed her. But Mrs Haye would give her a fine funeral with a stone which would have an angel on it maybe. Beautiful she always thought they looked, them tombstones as had angels on 'em.

And when she was gone Master Johnnie would be still more alone and he was lonesome enough now. He hadn't a soul left as belonged to him except Mrs Haye and her. The master had been the only son of an only son so that if Master John did not marry the name would go. Mrs Haye had brothers and sisters, and many of them, but they wouldn't speak to her nor she to them. It had been a romance her marrying the master. Mr William had told her at one time and another what he had heard at table and it seemed as if her parents had not approved of her marrying the master, and he as fine a man as ever was. The marriage had been sudden enough certain. So that when she had married against their orders, as it might be, they wouldn't hear of her again. That was a shame. Scotland she came from and lived in a fortress, they was wild them parts. But there it was and he was alone poor Master John. It was funny how some families did seem to die out, and when you thought of her own sisters and brothers dead and gone now and their children. There was no sense or order in it.

There was Christmas coming and she would have to begin thinking of what he would like. Two presents each year he got, one from Mrs Haye and one from her and every year he gave her one. To think of his having no one else to give him one. And it was hard to think of something he would want and it took longer to make things up now

147

as you were older. It had better be something warm, there was a hard winter coming, and she would make socks for Eliza's new baby her great-niece. He would want another muffler on cold days like this, and there would be more of them too, but then he would be wearing it with that hussy. What the world was coming to. To think of him walking out with her, that common thing.

And he had had a letter from that nurse only the other day, that was another one, stuck up she had been and not fit to look after anyone much less Master John. But he hadn't liked her, oh no she knew her Master Johnnie he didn't hold with her sort, and quite right too. The good Lord knew what she was. She hadn't liked to trust him a moment out of her sight when she was there. And she that would not take her meals in the hall and her no better than anyone. What did she think herself she would like to know. Oh it had been a mess-up everybody knocked off their feet, as it might be, by this happening. Mr William hadn't known which way to turn and it was the first time as she had seen him flustered. And she had not slept so much as a wink in three nights nor had cook with thinking of what he would want to eat what time he came back from hospital. Mr William had not known such a thing happen ever, and he was a knowledgeable man. And Mr Weston had worried himself about the fruit that he could 'ave peaches and grapes so that old Pinch could not remember anything like it ever, not that he was liable to, useless rude old man that he was. There had been the time when he had said to her quite sudden like "I ain't a-goin' to die yet awhile so don't you worry" which was all on account of her asking of him kindly as to 'is health, which no one could take offence at. But he was of the sort as drop down sudden. And there was Annie, poor body that was half-crazed, and for a week, when they had told her she said nothing but "Deary me" she felt it too poor soul, of course she did, as if they wasn't all fond of Master John. It was a mess-up.

But with Christmas coming on you really didn't know where you were, what with the happenings and everything, though it was all settling down now. But there was this girl he was walking out with which didn't bear thinking of. She would knit him a muffler that would keep him warm and there wasn't many as knitted as close and firm as she did if she didn't go quite so fast. And the socks for Eliza's new baby, Harriet they was going to call her and a good name it was, grandma had been a Harriet. Then there was Joe who was to marry next month, he would want a wedding present, something useful as would be a standby. He was a good boy that and a good son to his mother, her twin, as was dead now. Twelve brothers and sisters, the good Lord had been favourable to her mother, and six of them dead and gone now and four nephews killed in the war one after the other. But there was eight left. Joe had been too young to go, but now he was marrying and was in a good position, and there would be children and she would knit them socks . . .

She sipped. The kettle threw out sprays of steam and bubbles bubbled angrily about the lid. Sometimes the lid would rise as if to let something out, and there would be a hissing in the fire and then it would fall back again. The room was full of movement with sudden still glowing colours here and there on the furniture where the fire caught it. A late fly dozed just within the half-circle of light thrown out by the fire on the ceiling and where the shadows crept up from the corners trying to choke the light. The room was so warm. And the figure in the chair sat straight and quiet with hands crossed on her lap, and the whalebone in her collar kept the chin from drooping.

★   ★   ★

"So we are going to Swan's Wood, are we?"
"Yes, do you mind?"

149

"No."

He pressed closer.

"This silence with the sun and with the sharpness of the frost still on the ground and with you here . . ." he said, but she did not answer.

"The breadth and distance there is in the country to-day, June, don't you feel it?"

"I don't know."

"The country is so full of the sun to-day, June, and I am away from them all, for you have rescued me from the house, so that I am with you. And we have hours of time, this will be the longest walk of all that we have had yet. It is such an adventure. Do you like walking with me, June?"

"Perhaps I do, perhaps I don't."

"But you must, or else it will be so dull for you. And you are kind to take me out, for they are old in that house, so old. Poor Nan who is dying, and William the butler who is waiting for a pension, and old Pinch who is going to retire next week. Mamma is giving him a cottage rent free. He has worked in the garden for forty years."

"Do they get pensions? How much?"

"Enough to live on, when they have deserved it. But listen to that cock, June, crowing so boastfully such miles away. And the car droning up Bodlington Hill on its way to Norbury, with the stream just near hurrying by over the stones. And the birds are singing to the fine day, there are so many of them. Do you know the names of birds?"

"No, an' I wish I did."

"Nor do I, it does not really matter. But what luck that we should have the sun for our walk. We have had so much rain up to now."

"An' I hate rain."

"So do I! Listen to the starlings on that tree, screaming at us, perhaps. June, did you say the other day that you lived alone with your father?"

"Yes. Why not?"

"I did not mean that. It is a very excellent thing to do. But you must be very lonely sometimes."

"Sometimes."

"Then do you never see anyone? It must be so dull: I know how it is."

"Oh yes, I see one or two." She laughed.

"Who? But I never see anyone, except stewed people that Mamma serves up, when there is no way of keeping them out. And you are nicer than any of them."

"You are a funny card."

"Am I? Well, there are worse. things to be. Isn't it funny, though, that we should never have met in all these years? I have never seen you, June, never seen how you are."

"You have, only you don't remember. In church I used to watch you when we were both quite little, but you would hardly ever look at me, you were too grand. And afterwards."

"But then I must have seen you. Why did you look at me?"

"There was nothing else to do."

"No, I suppose not. Where did you sit?"

"To the left of your pew, just in front of the font. Don't you remember?"

"And what was the church like? I never really noticed it. Oh, it hurts to try and remember. I can only see bits of it, the spaces are so hard to fill up."

"Don't. I hate that church too, only through the window on the right you could see an apple tree."

"Yes, I know. And there were birds."

"And apples in the autumn. Do you remember?"

"Yes. Apples." And he laughed.

"Why do you laugh?"

"I don't know. But I did hate being made to go to church – though of course your father used to preach really well."

"Oh yes!"

"Mamma . . . He grew roses up the church, I think. I liked that very much. They were so pretty."

"An' Mrs Haye made him take them down again."

"Did she? I wonder why. Do you like roses?"

"Very much. There used to be so many of them in that garden at the old Vicarage. Father was always crazy on them, an' so was I."

"The rose is lovely, June, don't you think? The poets sing so often of them. They call her the queen of flowers. 'The damask colour of thy leaves.' 'Sweetness dwells in rosy bowers.' 'The blushing rose.'"

"Oh yes. They were all over our garden."

"Then you must have lived in a way dear to the lyrical poets of the seventeenth century. How charming!"

"I never read poetry. I haven't time."

"Really? And the church must have been so pretty, buried in them. But then Mamma is very low church."

"How do you mean?"

"Well, she does not like ornaments to a church. I think it is very silly of her, though Crayshaw goes too far with his lighted candles and so on."

"But what does it matter?"

"It is popery, that is all. It is going to Rome."

"What's that?"

"Oh well, why talk about it?"

"Father was so fond of his roses. Making him take them down like that was a shame."

"Listen to those bells, June. The sound comes tumbling over the country from so far off. It would be Purley church, I suppose."

"Father hates church bells. They hurt him."

"Where are we now?"

"We are just coming to Mr Brownlee's farm."

"I thought so. Brownlee's chickens are making such a noise."

It was a shame the way they had treated Father.

"What a lovely material your dress is made of."

"Do you like it?"

"So much. It is so soft, one's hand glides over it and then sinks down in the folds of it drowned in it, June. What colour are you wearing?"

"Blue."

"Yes, it would be blue."

"Poor boy, not being able to see."

"Call me John, dear, 'boy' is so young."

"Poor John."

"It has been awful without you."

"Has it?"

"Everything is black. Before, even when one shut one's eyes the eyelids were red if one were outside, but light now has been cut off from within. Nothing but black. One gets desperate sometimes, you know. There are times when I would like to kill myself, really, I mean."

"Poor John."

"But your eyelids when you closed them would be such a delicious colour for the lovely eyes inside."

"Would they? Oh, but then you have never seen my eyes."

"Perhaps not, but I can feel them just the same."

"Do you?"

"Yes, they are so calm, so quiet. Such a lovely blue."

"But they are dark brown."

"Oh. Then your dress does not match?"

"No, I suppose not."

"But what does that matter? They are such lovely brown eyes. And sometimes they light up and burn, perhaps?"

"How do you mean?"

"Well . . . But have you ever been in love?"

"I don't know."

"Maybe they are burning now?"

"N-no, I don't think so."

"How sad. And mine, if they had not been removed, would have burned so ardently."

"What's ardently?"

"You know, hotly, pas—No." This was awkward. "But I like your eyes, whether they are brown or blue."

"You are really quite nice, John, an' I think I like you."

"No more than that?"

"Perhaps."

And his hand was in hers. Better to ignore it at first.

"Perhaps?"

"Well, I don't know."

"You are strange, June, so distant, so cold. I don't believe you really like me at all, no, really not."

"Mind, here's a gate. Be careful."

"Where is the gate? You are cruel, you know. You don't care a bit. Oh, here it is; good."

"Care about what?"

"What about? Why, me, I mean. But this will be where we have to cross the road. Then we go through the gate which should be to the right there. Shut this one; that is the home farm we are leaving."

"Have you got a farm all of your own?"

"Yes, and why not?"

"You must be rich."

"I am not so sure about that."

"It must be wonderful to be rich."

"It must be wonderful to be poor."

"How do you mean? You've never been poor in all your life. So how can you tell?"

"But poor people are always much happier than rich people on the cinema. The cinema used to be the only way I had to see life."

"But what do you think of scrubbing floors all day, and of cooking food, and of having to look after your father who is ill, and all that?"

"Is he ill, June?"

"Yes, at least he thinks he is."

"I'm sorry. But you won't always be poor?"

"As far as I can see."

"But one day a fairy prince may spirit you away to a place of luxury. Think of it."

"Gracious, no! Why should he?"

"He would have every inducement. These things often happen, you know, here and there."

"I don't think so."

"But I do. One of these days . . . we . . . perhaps. Well; but I am so sorry he is ill."

"Oh, I don't think he is as ill as all that. He is a poet an' imagines things."

"A poet? Does he write poetry?"

"Yes. Leastways he doesn't write, but he talks beautiful. About stars and things. I can't understand him half the time, so I just say 'Yes' or 'No' to keep him company. He is a wonderful man."

"And you must lead a most thrilling life all alone with a poet in that house. Mamma says that the garden was – is very beautiful."

"Yes, it is full of trees and things."

"So wild. Such a free life."

"Free? Well, I don't know about that. But we have some chickens, only they have to be fed. And there's the cat. She killed a great big mouse the other day."

"Did she!"

"Yes, an' there's the chicks that get lost in the grass, I love them, an' there's a starling that nests every year in the chimney, and my own mouse which plays about in my room at night, an' . . ."

God, the boredom of this.

". . . but sometimes I hate it all."

"It must be horrid for you."

"I've had no one else to tell it all to."

"No, of course not. June, here we are in the wood. Do

you feel the hollowness of it? For the trees crowd about us, and their branches roof us in slyly, with sly noises that one can just hear. And we seem to be in another world now, for the cart that is creaking along the road outside is so faint, floating through the twigs that urge the sound gently along as they are tickled by the wind. So that we might be on our way to some dark and dangerous spot. June, it is mediæval."

"What's that?"

"It means long ago. But we are happy together, aren't we? You know, you are the only person I would take with me to Swan's Wood."

There was Mummy, but she did not count.

"Why?"

"Because I used to spend so much of my youth at the top there, thinking great thoughts."

"But why only me?"

"Surely you know."

"Perhaps I don't."

"Oh yes, you do."

"When I was little I used to tell everything to a friend I had then. We used to walk in the lane, down at Broadlands. One day she tripped up and cut her leg."

"And I have never told anyone everything."

"Tell me."

"I will some day, it would take too long now. June, are we getting near the top now?"

And he would tell her, it would help, though she would not understand. But he would never tell her of his writing, that was too important.

"I see light behind the trees."

"We are getting there. This must be near the top of the hill, and you are not a bit out of breath."

"My! an' here we are. Is that your view? I don't see much in it, not that it isn't very pretty though."

"Shall we sit down?"

"Yes."

She lets go of his hand and they sit down.

"June, give me back your hand, it makes you so much more real."

"There it is, silly."

"And what do you see of my view?"

"There are fields an' trees an' the river an' behind that the hill with the waterworks' tower an' to the right there is the town with the Abbey, no more than that."

"That is all gone for me, anyway. June, my hand is so comfortable in yours."

"Is it?"

"Yes. Your hand is warm and so strong. But it is only just big enough to hold mine."

"Shall we change round?"

"That is better. I have it captive now. It is like holding a bird."

"Oh you!"

"Oh me?"

"You are a funny boy."

"Do call me John."

"Funny John."

"How is your other hand, the one that was cut?"

"It is better now. But it did hurt."

"Poor hand. I was so sorry."

"Were you? That was nice. There was no one who cared."

"Poor June. But didn't your Father mind?"

"No, he never would. He is always thinking of himself."

"Well, he ought to have. It was . . ."

"No, no, he oughtn't, it wasn't his fault, he is a genius, you know. Great thoughts he has, not like you and me. Above it all."

Not like you and me!

"But, poor hand. Give it me, June. Ah, now I have both your hands – so much and yet so little."

"No, don't press it like that, you are hurting."

"How much would you give me of yours?"

"Of mine? Why? Well, I haven't very much to give. But if you like, I'll give you a brooch of my mother's which is broken so as I can't use it. You will remember me by that. But I expect you have a bad memory, John."

"Only when I have nothing to remember."

"What shall I give you, then?"

"What you like best."

"And what will you give me?"

"A ring, and more, perhaps."

"You are nice, John."

"Aren't I?"

"Oh, well, I never. Don't you ever think of me? It's always you, you, you."

"But, of course I think of you much more than you would believe possible. And you come to me in my dreams."

"John!"

"Yes, dear. It's true, even if I haven't told you before."

"How wonderful!"

"It is, and more than wonderful!"

He laughed, and there was a pause.

"No, it's not comfortable, your holding both my hands."

"Here is one back, then."

"John, the sun's come out and the Abbey has gone all gold."

"And it has caught the trees as well, perhaps? When the sun came out for a moment it used to be a great thing for me, and I have sat here entranced, but when you think that all this doesn't bother itself about one at all, it is a trifle boring."

"John, you are very like Father."

"Am I? How?"

"I don't know. You talk the same."

"Do I? Oh, well. But I used to dream here so. Have you never dreamed, June – about things, I mean?"

"Yes, perhaps."

"And what do you do all day? There must be time to dream."

"Oh, there's lots to do. But I do dream."

"What about?"

"I don't know."

"And this place would fit in with my mood. A view helps, do you find that?"

"Yes."

"At last, something definite. You really think that?"

"I suppose I do, seeing as how I said it."

"You are frightened of your feelings. But one soon grows out of that. I did a year ago."

"An' then there is the river. I sit on the bank sometimes an' watch it going by."

"I know. I love doing that. Do you fish?"

"No, I don't know how to."

"I used to, but I can't now."

"Poor John."

"Poor me. But it will not be 'poor me' if you are nice."

"But aren't I being nice?"

"Fairly."

"Well, I never! Only fairly? What more do you want?"

"Lots more."

"You are a one. But it is nice up here."

"With you. Say 'with you.'"

"Why should I? No, I won't."

"Say 'with you.'"

"No – hi, stop! What are you doing? If you go on like that I shall go home."

"But you didn't say 'with you.'"

"Why should I?"

"To please me."

"I'm not sure I want to now."

"Do."

"I'm sure I don't see why I should. But as you seem to've set your heart on it, here it is – 'with you,' stupid."

"It has no meaning now; how sad. You are very cruel, June. I used to think of cruel ladies and of kind ones when I was up here, but they were none of them like you."

"Cruel ladies and kind ones? What do you mean?"

"Such as one used to see on the cinema. I used to grow so romantic over this view. I wanted to go into politics then. When you thought of all the people starving, there was nothing else to do. I became Prime Minister, of course, up here, and addressed huge meetings which thundered applause. Once, at one of those meetings, a lady became so affected by my words that she had a fit. She was carried out, and the commotion over it gave me time to drink a cup of water, which was most necessary. It was all very vivid up here. I was to lead a public life of the greatest possible brilliance. It is different now."

"How wonderful that would be."

"You know what I mean? One planned everything out on a broad scale, remembering little scraps of flattery that someone or other had been so good as to throw one and building on that. One was so hungry for flattery. The funny thing is that when one goes blind life goes on just the same, only half of it is lopped off."

"Yes?"

"One would think that life would stop, wouldn't you? But it always goes on, goes on, and that is rather irritating."

"My life's always the same."

"Yes, I was on the crest of my audience and the woman threw her fit just as the climax was reached; but I repeat myself. I shan't feel that sort of thing any more now, there is so little to want."

"Oh, John!"

"And it would have been so lonely without you."

"Would it?"

"Say you like being up here with me."

160

"All right, so long as it pleases you."

"Pleases me? Only that?"

How slow, how slow this was.

"Oh, well. Nice boy."

"Thanks. But now, do you know what I am going to do now? After all, one must have something to put against one's name. For I am going to write, yes, to write. Such books, June, such amazing tales, rich with intricate plot. Life will be clotted and I will dissect it, choosing little bits to analyse. I shall be a great writer. I am sure of it."

"Yes."

"But I will be. What else is there to live for? Writing means so much to me, and it is the only thing in which the blind are not hampered. There was Milton."

"Ah yes, Milton."

"I must justify myself somehow."

"Funny John."

"Yes, very comical. Blundering about in the dark yet knowing about everything really. I know I do. And I will tell the world."

"Yes."

"But do you understand?"

"Yes."

"You see, June, no one cares enough, about the war and everything. No one really cared about my going blind."

"Yes."

"And I will write about these things – no one cares and I will be as uncaring as any. I will be a great writer one day, and people will be brought to see the famous blind man who lends people in his books the eyes that he lost, and . . ."

Poor John, he was properly off it now. She did not understand all this writing stuff; and how did one do it, it would be so difficult when one could not see the page?

". . . but I am boring you."

"No, you're not. Do go on."

"It is getting cold out here."

"Oh, don't let's go home just yet."

"So you like being out here?"

"Yes."

Why had he told her about his writing? Now everything was spoilt. And of course she did not understand. She was lamentably stupid. They had better go home.

"But you will catch a chill."

"Why should I? We can make each other warm."

And she pressed closer to him, and she laughed.

She would call that snuggling, he thought. There was a pause.

"John," she said, pulling his arm, "how silent you are."

"I have just said so much."

"How do you mean? Oh, John, will you write about me?"

"Perhaps."

"Fancy me being in a book. Just think."

"Would you like to be?"

"Of course I would. Father writes books too, only they never get written."

"Does he put you in them?"

"Oh no, they are not that sort."

"What sort are they?"

"I don't know. But he's always talking about his writing." She paused. "John, you'll make me the person your hero's in love with, won't you? and your hero'll be you, I suppose?"

"Perhaps."

"You aren't very chirpy now, are you, John?"

"No, it is cold out here."

"But don't I keep you warm?"

"It is my other side that is so cold."

"Well, an' perhaps we'd better go home."

"Yes, perhaps we had better go home."

They get up. He staggers, then, arm in arm, they go down the hill through the wood.

"Mind, John, there's a fallen tree here."

"Thanks. Where? Oh, here. June, how sad it is going home."

"Yes, it is. But we'll go out again."

"Of course."

CHAPTER III

Finishing

"How minute we are."

"Why?"

"Well, this does not seem to be a time of great feelings, perhaps we have had too many of them lately. And we are so small compared to the trees. Gods come and go, but trees remain. By 'small' I don't mean 'in height.' They seem to me so lasting, so grave in their fat green cloaks, or in winter like naked lace."

"There, an' I've forgotten to feed the chickens."

"We are so petty, while time in the towns rolls by on well-oiled wheels with horrible efficiency. The machinery there goes on and on, and there are bits of it that are not right. The most horrible injustices."

"There's no justice."

"No, there is no justice."

A long way beneath something in the town was dropped with a clang, while a tug coming up the river whistled to get through the lock, a long shriek which shivered through the trees. Birds circled in specks round the Abbey tower. There was no wind and on the hill smoke from a cottage fire drifted straight up towards the blue sky, for the sun was shining. Just in front, in the meadow by the edge of the wood, a rabbit was feeding quietly, trembling at being alive. And they sat together against a tree, he with his head on one side to catch what was going on, and she dozing, with the world drifting in and out of her mind.

"I hate this easy life with the millions toiling there."

"I don't find it easy."

"No, I suppose not. But I will do something, even if I am blind."

She pulled a wisp of hair away from her face and rearranged the ragged scarf about her neck.

"I expect you will, John."

"Do you think so?"

"Yes, I do."

A confused shouting came from the lock, into which the barges were being packed. Several dogs were barking at each other while men ran about. The rabbit sat up and listened.

"John, there's a darling rabbit out there," and the rabbit fled.

"Oh?"

"He's gone now."

"Oh?"

And they were silent. From the other side of the wood a ploughman cried to his horses. Then from in front came a rattling of machinery and the lock gates creaked, painfully slow.

"Why are you so silent to-day, John?"

"I must go, I must go away."

"What do you mean, away from here?"

"No, to the towns."

"Yes, I know. You do want to get off sometimes. So do I. Minnie is getting very tiresome, he's been making messes all over the house, an' father does hate messes. I really don't know what to do."

"What is Minnie?"

"Our cat."

"Why do you give him a female name?"

"I don't know. Father always calls him she. Father hates cats."

She had told him this before.

"An' Father's so nervy nowadays, you don't know what to do with him. It gets harder and harder to live there at all. Father spends so much money on – on small things we don't need. There often isn't enough to eat an' . . ."

He heard a train snort in the distance like a dragon, and the wood round reared itself in tall crowding shapes and dark images. A voice droned complaint and he saw a little figure at the foot of an image throwing words at the things which hemmed her in.

". . . but he doesn't care, he never thinks of me, it's me who has always to be thinking of him, how to keep him alive, how to keep the home round his head, how to manage so's he won't starve. Always thinking of him, I am, and he with never a thought to me."

"Poor June."

"Yes, it is poor June. You don't know what it is with your easy life down there. There's times when you don't know if your own life's safe when the fit is on him, he's so dangerous."

"June, he doesn't attack you?"

"Attack me? If you could see my – the bruises on my arm, you simply wouldn't believe. And he was brought to it, brought to it."

"I must go away."

"It wasn't his fault."

"We ought all to go away for a time. The country is poisoning us, June. Under all the smiles that one hears and the soft kindness that one sees at first, there is so much cruelty. We will go."

"They brought him to it."

"It's all so different in the towns, there is so much more going on."

"But I don't want any more to go on. I've got enough as it is."

"I'm so sorry."

"Oh, it's all right. If it wasn't for Father's being as he is, it wouldn't be bad. He's worse than usual just now, and he won't have you do anything for him."

"We shall never do any good in the country. What is the use of staying down here? I ought to go away."

"But how can we?"

We? How awkward!

"I shall ι.ever do any writing down here. It's no good, one can't."

"No, I don't suppose so."

"Does nothing ever happen in the country?"

"Well, I don't know that you have much to complain of, poor darling."

"What, you mean going blind like that? Yes, I had forgotten. Except for that, then, nothing has happened. Sometimes I see a pool shut in by trees with their branches reflected in the stagnant water. Nothing ever moves, the pool just lies there, day and night, and the trees look in. At long intervals there is a ripple; the pool lets it die. And then the trees look in the same as before."

"Funny John."

"I may be, but that is the country."

"D'you know how I live in that house where there's everything to clean, and with not a soul to help me, mind you, with a man that throws anything away, anywhere, an' the chickens to feed and the meals to cook?"

"There would be food to prepare and boards to scrub in towns."

"Oh, I know there would, but we could have a gay time there, what with dancing an' nice dresses an' everything."

"Oh yes, we could have a gay time there."

How different this was to the first time he had sat at the top with her a fortnight ago. Only two weeks and so many things had happened.

"You will take me, won't you, John darling?"

"Yes."

Let in for it this time.

"But I can't leave Father."

"But I thought you said you wanted to go."

"I wanted to make sure of you. Besides, why can't I make believe?"

"Don't you want to go with me, then?"

"Yes. But I can't leave Father, he wouldn't be able to do anything without me. Poor Father, he's helpless, you know. He must have someone to look after him. And anyway you'ld have gone off."

"June, why do you say that?"

"They always do. There was a story I read called *The Love of White Hope*. The young man in that left his girl whom he had promised to marry, and she committed suicide, which was stupid, and he was so sorry that he drank water for the rest of his life, or something, I forget, which was stupider still. Yes, that was it, he used to drink in his young days, and then after that he gave it up. He was lovely when he was young. You would never take me with you."

"But I asked you to come."

"Did you?"

"I said you could."

"But you never meant me to."

"Yes, I did."

"I know you didn't."

"Why don't you come, anyway? It will not be for long, probably."

"Shall I?"

A cow bugled dejectedly. He thought that the neck would be stretched out with the mouth half open as though it were going to vomit. Idiotic cows.

"No, I can't leave Father."

"Well, don't say now that I didn't ask you."

"But you never meant me to go."

Another cow answered from a long way off, and they exchanged dull grief across the hedges and the meadows. The hedges would be black at this time of the year, and the trees bare. The plough creaked leisurely, how slow everything was.

168

"I'm not blaming you. You're not the sort that are meant to stay. Your sort can get rid of anything that displeases them, as Father says."

"June, do come."

"No."

"Then I don't see what you have to complain of from me."

"Poor John."

"It's not as if you are going to have a baby or anything."

"Don't."

"Well, is it?"

"You don't understand."

There was a long pause.

"Oh, to be in a town again, to hear a barrel-organ, for instance, across the street through gaps in the traffic! And all the rush there, and the thousands of people. I'd give anything to be there and just listen, so much would be going on, while here . . ."

"I couldn't leave Father, could I, now?"

"No, perhaps not. But I think it is really fine of you to stay with him, I really do."

"Fine? I don't know about that."

"Well, I mean, if he attacks you. And he has not done a great deal for you."

"It isn't his fault – besides, I won't have you say things like that about him. Anyway I shouldn't have been here if it wasn't for him."

"I am sorry. I did not mean that. Certainly I have much to be grateful to him for."

"Why, how do you mean?"

"For your being here."

"Nice John."

Why had he made a compliment like that? And why had she swallowed it?

"What will you do, June?"

"I don't know."

She never knew, perhaps that was the best. But he was beginning to.

"Well, remember, if ever you want to run away, come up to London and stay with us. We have not yet arranged to go to London; that is, I have not even broached the subject with Mamma, but I must go, and in the end she and I will go. So just you come when you want."

"I will. An' may I bring Father too?"

"But – but yes, if you think he needs it."

"I know you. An' what's wrong with Father? He's nothing to be ashamed of. You think I don't notice the way people pass us as if we weren't there when they meet us on the road. It's not his fault his being what he is. He was brought to it, and by your lot too."

"June, what do you mean?"

"They were always criticising him – d'you suppose I don't know how it was? – always carping away at him till his life wasn't his own and as if it didn't belong to him and no one else, and not to everyone as they thought, and finding fault with Mother for being in love with the postman, of course it was wrong, but why shouldn't she, and them saying that he didn't do his duty by the parish when he was worth the whole crew of them put together."

"But, June . . ."

"Oh, I'm not blaming you, don't be frightened. But it was your lot that brought him to it, it . . ."

These scenes. And after all, flirting with the postman, it was unfortunate, and a squalid story. Now the man was so soaked in the whisky, or whatever it was he drank, that he was a topic of conversation. For that alone one ought to be grateful to him. But Mamma was right for once, it was disgraceful. But it was sad too.

". . . poor, poor Father."

"Yes, June, I am so sorry."

"You aren't really."

There was a pause, and then he said:

"I think perhaps suffering is rather fine, don't you?"

Was it? He did not know. At any rate, it was a way out of blindness. She began again:

"But why wasn't I allowed to wear nice dresses and stay in the Vicarage and go to dances an' have some fun? Why have I got to scrub floors all day and cook meals and look after the house with never a word of thanks? It isn't fair."

"But you and I are really rather lucky . . ."

"Lucky? You . . . ?"

His face, that awful face. He didn't know what scars he had, poor boy. You couldn't say anything to him, with his blindness an' all.

". . . but not *lucky*, John."

"I can't express myself. And I cannot understand how you endure your life if you don't see the fineness in its being as it is."

"Endure it? Why, it just goes on. Oh, John, you will take me with you, won't you?"

"What is going to happen to Mr Entwhistle, then?"

"I can't leave Father."

"Does he want to go to the towns?"

"No, he says that would be running away, I don't know what from, though."

"You couldn't leave him, June."

"No."

"But you will one day."

"How do you mean? When he dies? Oh no, he mustn't die."

"I wish you saw that about suffering."

What could one say to her? If one was in her position and did not make it into something, it was not worth its own unpleasantness, that must be so. So that if she was too small to understand, she had much better go on the streets and have a good time on and off, if she could get it no other way. She could not come to London with him, even if they went there, for she would only be unhappy. He could never introduce her to his friends, if he educated her she would only be genteel. Her value was her brutality, and she would lose that. Besides, there was the Shame, who was a fool from all accounts, almost an idiot. But you couldn't let her go back to him in this frame of mind, it was waste. And what would she do when the old man died? – not that he was old, either, but quite young. Probably marry a commercial traveller. He would talk to Mamma. Oh, he was tired, tired.

There was a roar in the distance.

"June, what was that?"

"It's a football match on the Town ground. Norbury are playing Daunton to-day, so Mrs Donner told me. She has a son that plays, wonderful they say he is."

"That must have been a goal, then. Or a foul."

"Oh, John, you mustn't go."

"Where?"

"Why, to London, of course. What shall I do?"

A huge voice came as a whisper from across the river. "'ere!" it said, frenziedly, "'ere!" And another roar overwhelmed it, then a shrill whistle, and silence.

"It is no good, June, I must go. And June must go too, if there is anything in a name. Think of your August, and of how exciting that will be. It will come right one day."

"Will it?"

"You see, you cannot leave your Father; what would he come to? It is your duty to stand by him. It is good for one, too."

How unpleasant it was giving this sort of good advice. She ought to stay down here, from every point of view it was best that she should. And when the man died he would see what could be done. Yes, he really would.

"We will write to each other, June, and everything will seem better to-morrow."

"It won't."

"Yes, it will. Poor June. But think, we have had one

good time anyway, you and I, haven't we? There is one good thing behind us anyway, isn't there?"

"Don't go, don't go-o."

God, she was weeping. Well, that had finished it, he could not go. Poor June, and what a beast he was.

"All right, June, I won't go. It's all right, June, I'm not going. I'm not going, June, so it's all right."

"I'm so mis-erable."

"But I am not going."

"It's" (sniff) "not that."

"Aren't you glad I am not going?"

"No. Yes."

"Well, then?"

Why did one always talk baby-talk to someone who was crying?

"There, June, are you better now?"

"Yes." Sniff. "The chickens'll be starving." Sniff. "I'd better go home."

"Oh, you must not go home yet. June, I love you so."

"Do you?" Sniff.

"Yes, I . . ."

"But, John, I think you'd better go to London, after all. It'll be better for you there. I was only crying because of everything. I'm better now . . ."

What did she mean? What was in her mind? What was this, what was this?

". . . fond of me, and I must help Father with his book, his wonderful book which will come out next year, we're hoping. An' you'll go to London and do whatever you're going to do there, I know you will. I expect you will be a great man one day. There's the chickens. I've got to feed them an' look for eggs, too, for supper. Shall I walk you back or can you get home alone now? For I've got to hurry."

"No, I can get back alone all right by the roads. But,

June, don't go like this. What does it mean, – I mean how do you . . . ?"

"Oh, you go to London. Father an' I've got the book to write. He'll show you all what a mistake you made. So long, John."

"Good-bye, Joan."

Another roar came from the football crowd, an angry sound. A dog had been barking monotonously for ever so long.

"But, June," he shouted, to the wood, "June, what do you – June, I – June . . ."

But there was no answer, and he began feeling his way down the ride. How strange it all was, what could she mean? One's head felt in an absolute turmoil, one didn't know what to think.

He felt ill.

★   ★   ★

Heavy clouds lay above the house, mass upon mass. From the garden rose a black tangle of branches with showers of wandering twigs. And on these would hang necklaces of water-drops caught from the rain, shining with a dull light. Over the river in the dark pile of wood there showed frightened depths of blue, untrusting patches of it, lying here and there. The grass on the lawn was sodden, beaten to a lake of pulp. But over everything was a freshness of morning and of rain that had gone by, and there was a feeling that the trees and the house and the sky were washed, and that this day was yet another page, that there were more to be, so quiet it was.

She came down the stairs, pausing at the hole on the ninth step, and entered the kitchen, a song on her lips. The room was filled with a wet, grey light that made it kind, and she was happy, so that she thought of sweeping the floor. Father had been much better lately, those pains of his had gone, and perhaps he had been drinking less. How would he be to-day? It was not good for him, all the gin he drank, but he could not help it. How nice it was this morning. She was sleepy, so sleepy. A wonderful dream last night, about a young man who had made love to her, with blue eyes. Poor John. But it was dusty in here. She went to the cupboard under the stairs and took out the broom.

The broom swept a wrinkle of dust across the floor, with matches and crumpled paper and dried mud thrusting along together in it. She hummed contentedly and thought about her poor John. Her poor John who had no eyes. Blindness would be a terrible thing to come upon you, and he was so brave about it, always talking as if it were nothing. You couldn't help liking that in him. Oh, it was so wonderful this morning, and he was wonderful too. He was a gentleman, just as they themselves were for that matter, it was birth that counted, besides he hadn't treated her as anything else but the same as himself. But there was no going on with him. It wasn't as if times weren't difficult enough just with her own set of troubles, his into the bargain were too much. Though if she had gone with him it would have been a score over Mrs Donner. And what would have become of Father then? He had been so much better lately, quite different from what he had been before. Where was Minnie? And she hustled the dust through the door, driving it into the air in a fan-shaped cloud till it settled on the grass round the flakes of mud and the paper and matches which sat there taking a first look round.

Now there was no nonsense about George. How those cows did eat, all day long, and when they weren't eating they were chewing over again. And George had been quite nice lately. He had even said something, rather surly and rude, and she had been rude back. At any rate it was a beginning. Funny George, he was so powerful, his hands looked as if they could hurt you so, not like John with that awful face always screwed up with his scars; you were frightened of him in a horrid way. John was clever right enough, but there wasn't much to those clever ones. While George could do anything with those hands. The beech tree looked very big this morning, with the damp lying on his trunk in sticky patches. But the weather was clearing, and it felt so fresh this morning. There were the chickens to feed. Roses, roo–zez, all the way.

Getting some grain out of a cupboard in the kitchen, she went to the hut and let the chickens out. The cock was quiet and dignified this morning, rather sleepy. But as soon as he was in the yard he challenged the world and then scratched over a stone. The hens at once began to bustle about anxiously. When June scattered the grain they hurried to each fresh handful, while the cock asserted himself in the intervals of eating. She laughed at them as she always did, and cried "Chuck, chuck," and they clucked back with choking voices.

She sauntered away and stood looking at the trees over the river. There had been a new man on the milk lorry yesterday, which was exciting. He had such a nice smile, and all for her as she leant over the gate. He would be going by again about half-past two, she would be there. Perhaps he had come for good, and had taken the place of the one with the wicked face. He had had two lives, that one. But the new man was a dream, with fair, fair hair and his blue eyes that danced. It was nice to have somebody new. There was a lot new to-day.

Funny how sometimes you suddenly saw everything different. The chickens looked just like old women going round to tea-parties, and the cock like that old Colonel who used to call Father "Padre." They were well out of that. That was John's life, and – well, he was done with, anyway. Three weeks and not a word, but then that was like him. Probably there would be three letters one after the other in a week's time, he was all moods. Nice the way the wind blew the sleep from off you.

Father's voice from the window: "Is breakfast ready?"

"In a minute."

"Oh, it's all right. Don't hurry."

"I won't."

Oh, why was she so happy to-day? And he was too, you could tell by his voice, he never spoke like that unless things were going well. She hugged her arms. The way that hawk hovered. Where was Minnie?

She called: "Minnie, Minnie."

He would turn up in a minute or two. He was always coming from nowhere, so to speak. You looked down and there he was, rubbing his back against your leg, quite uncanny it was.

She turned and went back into the house. There was Father coming downstairs.

"Breakfast isn't ready yet. I've had no time."

"That's all right. Let's go out."

"It's fine," he said, "this morning, fine."

They walked in silence along the path smothered in weeds. The dripping undergrowth was shining. A sparrow chirped. And there, suddenly, was Minnie.

"Oh, Minnie."

"So she has come out too. I don't hate her so much to-day. Puss, puss."

Darling Minnie, so sleek, and looking rather frightened of Father, the cold eyes watched him so closely. Webs of moisture clung to Minnie's coat, making such a brave show, pearls on black velvet.

"Minnie."

And he lifted a paw.

"Never mind, leave her alone. We've interfered with her hunting. Anyway she'll want to be killing. Come on."

That was a good sign, Father not making a fuss when he saw him. His head was redder than usual, too.

"What about this Haye?"

"Oh, we parted."

"Parted" had such a wonderful feel about it, and it had been so quiet. They had just said "good-bye."

"Good thing too."

"He was quite nice."

"I don't think much of that house."

They walked on, round and round the old lawn. She had a fluttering inside.

"How did you know, Father?"

"Mrs Haye wrote."

"Wrote? What to say?"

"That you were going out with him. What business was it of hers, what you were about?"

"She wrote to you?"

"Damn them all. But you would have done well to have married him. It meant money."

"But I couldn't leave you."

"Very good of you."

She felt a kind of clearness, she saw her way. She was much, much happier than ever. She took his arm, but he seemed so uncomfortable that she let it go again.

"What'll you do, d'you think?"

"Stay here."

"But you can't always do that, you know. You'd better go away."

"Where to?"

"But you'll marry some day."

"No, I'll stay with you."

He pressed her arm. This time she did not try to press his, he was so shy.

"And there's your book to write."

"Yes, my book."

There was a pause, and then he went on:

"I tell you what, I'll fix up that hen-run to-day. But then there is no rabbit wire, and it is so expensive. Oh, well."

"They're just as well as they are. Look, Minnie has just pounced."

178

"I must go and have a drop of something."

"Why not give it up for a bit?"

"Oh no, can't give it up, does one good, you know."

"Then I'll get breakfast ready."

He went through the kitchen and into his room while she began leisurely putting out the breakfast things. A sheet of chill winter sunlight lay on the floor, and some of it was spilled over the window frame as well. She dabbled her feet in it and it came up to her knees. In her hand was the teapot, and, in the other, half a loaf of bread. There came the sound of a cork being drawn in the next room, which sent a shiver pleasurably down her spine. It got rather dull here when he knocked off the drink. But still, it was bad for him. Turning, she put the things down on the table and then went over to the cupboard.

A cough came from the next room. Then the door opened and he came through, a faint flush over his face, and went out of doors. From outside he shouted through the window:

"It's great to-day."

And there were patches of blue sky. Oh, it was going to clear up. Was there enough milk? Yes, just. Anyhow he wouldn't get angry, not yet awhile, at any rate. Marry? Who was there to marry? No one as far as she could see. They were all too difficult or too easy. George was only something to do, if she hadn't had someone to think of she would have gone mad. That new milk-lorry man was so nice-looking. But she ought to stand by Father, it was easier that way. Why marry, anyway? It would all turn out right in the end.

Mrs Donner said that the other night when the wind had risen so, a tree had blown down across the road and had prevented Mrs Haye getting to Barwood without wetting her feet, and that was a good thing. What did she mean by writing to Father? She would like to marry John now, just to spite her. She poured milk out of the can into the teapot, and then began to wash up the plates from over-night.

179

Father did not like eating off dirty plates, and it wasn't really very nice either. She would have to change this water she washed everything in, it was so greasy that you couldn't do anything with it, and it smelt rather. They might as well have some of that tinned herring. They had eaten it once too often, but still it was good.

Father was better. He hadn't been like this in the morning for many a time. So pleasant to talk to, and he hadn't minded about breakfast. Yes, she would stay here and help him, he needed her, and look how much better he was already. And what would they do then? You didn't know. It was not as if he could have a living again. But he would find some job, sure to. She laid out the clean plates and put out the butter. Had a mouse or something been at it? They were devils, those vermin, they got into everything and ate all that they set eyes on. There was nothing to be done, you couldn't do away with them, there were too many. She put down the tin of herrings with the opener and looked contentedly at the table. She called:

"Father, breakfast is ready."

He came in slowly and sat down.

"I'm so lazy."

"So'm I," said she.

★   ★   ★

Mrs Haye was sitting in an armchair in her sitting-room reading a volume of reminiscences that some hunting man had left behind him. Over the fireplace Greylock looked down upon her, while on the writing-table stood Choirboy's hoof, and there were sporting prints on the walls and an Alken in the corner. But all round were masses of flowers, the air was heavy with the scent of them, for her one extravagance was the hot-house, and Weston understood flowers. This book was interestin', she had never known that the Bolton had distemper in '08 and mange in

180

'09, a most awkward time for them, and the bitch pack had been practically annihilated. Again, it appeared that in '13, Johnson, who used to hunt hounds so marvellously, had broken an arm, and on the very next day his first whip, the man that the Aston had now, had cracked his thigh. It was an unlucky pack. They had had foot-an'-mouth for two years now. Their own pack down here was gettin' impossible. Even the Friday country was infested with wire, which of course was young Beamish's fault; why they hadn't given the job to someone more experienced no one could tell, but then there was some money that went with it. And she would have to get rid of this groom of hers, Harry; he drank, there was no doubt about it, you had only to smell him. What could one do?

Mabel would be here soon, and then they could have a long talk about it all.

How dark it was getting. Putting aside the book she rang the bell. Really it was becoming most tiresome, this affair between Herbert and Mrs Lane. All day long they were at it, she had seen them again yesterday, spooning in the back yard. And the cooking suffered in consequence, that beef had been positively raw three days ago, and there seemed to be nothing but vegetables to eat now, John had been complainin' about it. His appetite had returned, which was splendid. Where was William? She and Mabel could really have the business out, she knew she would approve. Ah, at last.

"William, bring the lamps, please."

The old thing had aged lately. They were all gettin' older; and with Jennings dying like that, it was sad. Pinch retirin' too, the garden didn't look the same without him. But he was comfortable at home, and he had earned a rest.

There was somethin' the matter with Annie, perhaps she was getting really crazy, and they ought to send her to a home, but the other morning when she had said to her near the rubbish heap, with such a gleam in her eye, "There will

181

be new leaves soon," it really was too extraordinary. And what did she mean, it wasn't even March yet? Why were there always idiots in a village? And there was nothing one could do for them, that was the annoyin' part about it.

Here were the lamps. Appalling it was, the way some people were installing electricity, oil was much more satisfactory. They had always had oil and always would. Electricity was so hard and bright that it was bad for your eyes.

"William, Mrs Palmer will be in for tea to-day."

She was late, and that was wrong of Mabel, she knew how it irritated her to have to wait. She needn't have hurried so down from the village. That roof in Mrs Cross's cottage would have to be seen to, it was in a terrible state, she ought to have been told before. Would the next people take any trouble? But then that wasn't settled yet.

She was restless to-day, she hadn't been able to settle down to anything, this thing had been weighing on her mind so. And there were the household accounts to do, she was late with them, and they should be interesting this month. Mrs Lane would have been going through an orgy of waste, the affair with Herbert would be sure to make her careless. They would have to take sixpence off the income tax this time, things couldn't go on as they were, and the papers were full of it. Of course, giving this up would save money, but then there would be no flowers and no horses. So much of one would go with it. Mabel was late, late.

A motor. Ah, the Cadillac. Really, it was too bad of her, and it was not as if she ever had anything to do. Well, anyway, they could get down to business now.

The door opened.

"Mrs Palmer."

"My dear Emily, I'm so sorry I'm late. You see, my dear, the Cadillac broke down on the way, so tiresome of it. How are you?"

"Very well, thank you, Mabel dear; and you?"

They lightly kissed.

"I caught a nasty chill at the Owens' dance, and I've only just thrown it off. My dear, such a bore! There are nothing but draughts in that house, you know how it is. I think they might let one have one window shut, don't you? Emily, it is nice to see you, I haven't come across you for a week."

"To tell you the truth, Mabel, I haven't been about much this week. With the village and one thing and another I haven't had a moment. I wanted to have a talk . . ."

The door opened. John came in.

"Who is it?"

"Mabel, John."

"How are you, John?"

"Oh, is it you? I'm all right, thanks. How are things with you?"

"Well, you know how it is, dear boy, one irritating thing after another. Only this afternoon on the way here the inside of the car went wrong, so tiresome. We waited for hours while Jenkins tried to find out what was the matter. And while we were there guess who should come by at the most appalling speed, my dear, so that it was not safe for anyone." Pause. "The young Vincent boy on his motor bike."

"Was he going fast?"

"My dear boy, he shot by, I have never in all my life seen anything like it, you know."

"John dear, would you mind leavin' Mabel and me for a short time? We want to have a talk."

"Then I shall see you at tea, Mrs Palmer." The door shut.

"What has happened, Emily, nothing serious, my dear?"

"Mabel, I wanted to talk over a very important matter with you. You see, it's about John."

"What? He is not ill again or something?"

"Let us go straight to the point. Let me collect my thoughts. You see, Mabel, it's like this. But perhaps I had better begin at the beginning. You see, even before he went blind, I knew that he was not made for the country, you know how one can tell about one's boy. Well, anyway, from one thing or another I saw that he was not happy down here. You see, he has never liked huntin' or shootin' or any of those things, and now he can't fish. I don't know how it is, he is not in the least like Ralph or me. Where can he have got it from? And this writing that he is so keen about, of course I encourage it, my dear, it is so good for the boy to have a hobby, but no one has ever written on either side of the family. Ralph even found letter-writing almost impossible. So that it is so difficult to understand him, dear."

"Yes, Emily, I have always felt that, you know."

"And then one has had girls to the house so that he might see some nice young things, but he has never taken to any of them, Mabel. There was Jane Blandair, a charming girl, but he has told me, in confidence of course, that he definitely dislikes her. My dear, I asked him why, and he said that it was everything about her. What can one do? Jane would have made such a splendid wife and mother. And of the other girls who have been, there was not one of them I would not have liked for a daughter-in-law. And he is quite a catch, isn't he, clever and artistic, and he will have a little money. It was all very depressing, Mabel."

"Yes, dear, I felt for you so."

"Well, I was wretched about the whole business, and I slowly came to realise that he was not made for the country, like you or I. You see, he does not really care for the village, though he makes great efforts, poor boy. And then it is his future that matters. He gets terribly bored down here, he has no interests. He is always talking of the towns. He never actually says it, but I know he thinks we all get into grooves in the country, and so I suppose we do, I mean I personally am always fussin' about the village, but of course he is too young to realise that one gets into a groove wherever one is. But there is his writing. That is his only interest. He has been so very brave all through this business, and he is now writing as hard as ever he did; naturally I encourage it, I think everyone should have a hobby, and I am sure you agree with me in this, Mabel. But he seems to think that one can't write books in the country. Though all the books that you and I used to read, Mabel, like Jane Austen, were written about the country. Still, he thinks that he can't, and I have always told him to try, but it must be so different when one is blind. So what he wants is to go away, Mabel, that is what it all comes to. He has never said it, of course, but that is what he wants to do."

"To go away, Emily? What for?"

"Well, he is young . . ."

"Yes, but we all know the wretched life they live in town, you know how it is, dancing all night and only getting up for lunch, you know how it is. I never could stand it when I was a girl. My dear, I don't understand it."

"I think I do. I'm his mother, you see. He needs a change."

"Listen, Emily, why not take him to Eastbourne for a few weeks? Such air you get at Eastbourne."

"It is not that, besides there are other things. No, he – we must go to London."

"To London! For how long? But think of the noise. Do you mean for the winter and then come down here in the summer?"

"We could not afford it, Mabel. You see, so much of the money went in those shares which are worthless now. No, it would have to be for good."

"My dear Emily, no, I cannot allow you to do this, you know. No. Think of the Town Council, and the Board of Guardians, what would they do without you? All it would mean is that the Walkers woman would take charge of the whole thing, Colonel Shoton is such a hopeless creature. And think of the village, Emily. Oh, you can't go. It is probably only a passing whim of the boy's, you know.

Take him to Eastbourne to get over it, my dear. Don't do this thing recklessly. When you and I were young we had these moments ourselves when we wanted to get away. Why even now sometimes I say to myself that it is all too much and that I was happier at Allahabad, you know how it is, only a little restlessness, my dear."

"It's more than that, Mabel. I've been so wretched about the whole thing."

"Yes, my dear, I am so sorry for you, but don't let the fact of you being a little over-wrought influence you to . . . Why, think of the village. You know better than I do that Mrs Crayshaw is so busy having babies that she has absolutely no time to attend to the affairs of the village. Why, it would all be indecent and disgraceful if you went so that there was no one left to look after it. You know how it is, illegitimate babies immediately, my dear. Oh no, Emily, you cannot go. Besides, what does the boy want to do in London?"

"Yes, but you see he is artistic."

"But, Emily, painters always go to the country for inspiration. I have never heard of a painting of a town that was any good. And there is nothing to write about in a town. Don't let him ruin your life, Emily."

"My duty is by him."

"Yes, my dear, but does he know what he wants? He is only restless. And what would become of the committees and everything? And the Hospital Ball, Emily?"

"Yes."

"And the Nursing Association, and the Women's Institute, just when it is beginning to go so nicely, you know. Without you it would collapse. You are absolutely indispensable to its welfare!"

"Am I?"

"Now don't be modest. Why, of course you are. Think of Mrs Walkers on the Board of Guardians. Emily, she isn't honest."

"She is dangerous, that woman."

"My dear, do you know what I heard the other day? That as a very natural result of the way she goes on and what with all the money she burns and the way she keeps that house open always, trying to get people to come to it, you know how it is, and of course no one will, she is in the hands of the moneylenders. Deeply involved."

"Well, I don't know whether I should altogether believe that, but it is very interestin'."

"Isn't it? All it means is that she will be misappropriating funds as soon as you are out of the way. And you know I've no head for figures."

"Yes; well, I don't know."

There was a long pause while outside the night drew in softly, peering through the windows at the fire and the pools of light kept by the lamps. Mabel Palmer was lying back in her chair worn out by what she had had to say, and Mrs Haye was looking vacantly at Greylock. Presently she roused herself.

"Shall we have tea now, Mabel?" And she got up and rang the bell.

★　　★　　★

"Is everything in?"

"All that I'm going to take, yes."

"Well, I must go and see about the labels." Mamma hurried out again.

John stood in the middle of the room, smoking a cigarette. So they were going. Lunch had been a hurried affair, he had hardly eaten he was so excited. He had a wonderful stirring in his belly, for they were going. A light feeling, a warning of change. They had packed all that was being taken. When they got there Uncle Edward had lent them his house till they should find one for themselves. Everything was packed and arranged. There was only the train now. It was nice of Uncle Edward. He sat down on his trunk.

Was there anything more dreadful than waiting to be off? When there was nothing left to do, and you were forced to sit about and wait? He did not dare to walk for the positions of everything had changed, chairs were upside-down in the middle of what had once been a path, there was a large packing-case with protruding nails in what had been the passage between the sofa and the fireplace in the Hall, and he had tripped over a carpet which was rolled up suddenly for half its length. Desolation brooded over each room, and there were clouds of dust driving along here and there on draughts. The flowers had been removed so that the house was cold and hollow. It was changed.

For of course they were moving. London was only six hours off now. Life would be quite different when they got there. Barwood would be wiped out, and he was going to begin again, on the right path this time. Think of all that one would write when one got to London, great things were going to happen there. He would hunt out B. G. and Seymour; they would introduce him to all the amusing people. How nice it was to be going.

He had thought that yesterday was never going to end. Sitting here all the afternoon and all the evening, with William moving about painfully, stacking what he was to take away in one corner, and what was to be left and sold in another. Mamma had shot in and then shot out again continually, and her voice had been breathless at the number of things left to do, with a high note of anxiety whistling through her sentences. Ever since that day three months ago when she had sent him away that Mabel might deliberate alone with her, the high note had pierced through her conversation. Mabel had come many times since then, almost every day, and lately her voice had grown hard towards him, as if she thought that he was ruining Mamma's life. But after all he had not made the suggestion

188

first, it had been Mamma a month back who had said quite suddenly, "We are going to London," and he "To London?" "Will you like that, dear?" Everything inside him had been beating, beating. It was good of her. He had a sinking feeling now, the whole thing was almost too good to be true.

Spring was beginning here, and the hot rain that fell in short bursts made the room sticky. They said there was a haze of yellowy green over the black trees. He took off his tie and opened his collar.

Nothing had happened in those last three months, nothing had ever happened down here, or rather, nothing always happened. He had thought a good deal and little had come of it, only he had seen God as a great sea into which all goodness drained, and those who were good pumped the goodness out again and watered the desert to make the flowers grow. Trees drew it up. A pretty notion. And all the time expectancy had quivered in the air, making life unbearable, there had been so much going on behind the scenes. Poor William, he had been sad packing yesterday. He was not coming to London, he was too old, and he was retiring on a pension, like old Pinch. That was another thing, all the old people were being left behind to die, and Nan was dead. There would be a new start in London. Poor Nanny, but she was happy, nursing children who had died young. Would she remember him? On her character in heaven "Great experience of blind babies." Oh, he was so happy to-day.

But Mamma would be happy in London, she would meet there all the people she had known in Scotland before she had married, and they both wanted to get away from Barwood. A town would be a great hive of houses where people were born and lived and died bitterly, there would be no dozing as in Norbury. They would be in the centre of things there, they would be on the spot, and the echoes of what was happening that one only heard faintly in these muffled fields would be clear up there, as a gong. Life was only nice in retrospect, and they could look back on the mists that coiled round Barwood and make them into an enchanting memory, with Joan rising through them, attracting a stray glance of the sun, and dispelling the mists a little.

The coal fire burned steadily with a brittle tinkling sound, as though flakes of glass were falling tiny distances. Far beneath something groaned at being moved.

The train, the first time since the affair.. The same boy might sit and throw more stones, one of which might hit his window appropriately. Or there might be a collision, trains were unlucky for him. They would rush through the quiet fields while the telephone wires dipped beside them, over rivers where the fish lay under the bank, through villages where Barwood was repeated, through towns that were not big enough, till they crawled into the biggest town of all, dirtied by all the work that was going on there.

Far away a steamer whistled on the river, it was the first warning of change. He was so excited. The room was sticky with damp. The soft harping rain fell rustling, rustling, while from the eaves drops pattered down on to the window-sill.

Feet climbing stair carpet and Mamma came in.

"We're off in half an hour. Is everything ready?"

"Yes, I think so."

She went down the stairs, more slowly this time. Half-way down she paused to look at her watch, then hurried on.

"William, they ought to be off now, if they are going to catch that train. Are all the labels on?"

"Yes, madam."

One, two – five – seven, eight. Eight trunks. They were all there, piled on to two cars. Cars were so expensive to hire nowadays. Thirty shillings. Ruinous.

"Get in, Janet, get in. You have got the money I gave you? Don't forget to label them to Paddington. The stationmaster is expectin' you, and I will be there soon, so you'll be all right. Yes, drive away."

Janet waved to William. He had aged, he looked so worn standin' by the door there. It was a terrible business gettin' people off.

"There they go, madam."

"Yes."

What did he mean? Of course they were going. What?

"They have not stopped, William?"

"No, madam."

Janet was a capable young thing and she had travelled, so she would be able to manage. Besides, Smith had promised to look out for her.

"Are the labels on all the suitcases?"

"Yes, madam."

"Well, we start in half an hour."

Half an hour. Now what had she forgotten? Everything must be in. And anyway, Dewars would send her the inventory, so that she could send for anythin' she did not want to sell. They could come by the furniture vans.

"William, if there is anything I find missin', you will send it up in the vans with the furniture."

"Yes, madam."

Well, that was that. She sank into a chair. A great sigh escaped from inside her. How terrible a house looked when you were gettin' out of it. And all the doors were always left open. She got up and shut them, then she came back to her chair. This rain was horrible, and there was no fire. Had she said a word to everyone? Of course she was not going away for good, but they were not to live down here any more, so that a word or two was expected of you. It was so difficult, too, to find anythin' to say. She had loved them all, and they loved her, but they did not understand her going away like this. They were always asking who was going to live here instead, and she did not know. It was a relief, though, now that they were really off, now that those endless discussions were over. Mabel was impossible sometimes, this business had estranged them almost. The clock had stopped. Really, William might have wound it up, even if they weren't going to be here this evenin'. She looked at her watch. Twenty-nine minutes.

It was nice of Edward to lend them his house with the caretaker and his wife. The two would quarrel, of course, that was the trouble about having married servants, but they would be comfortable there, and it would give one time to look round. 9 Hans Crescent. A German name, but, after all, the war had been over some time. Nine. But . . . And she had only counted eight, and she had let them go off. What was this?

"William, William!"

"Yes, madam."

"Did you take Mr John's trunk?"

"Mr John? Mr John's box?"

"Oh, oh. I was afraid that would happen. I should have reminded you. Oh dear."

"Will you take it with you, madam?"

"Yes, that would be best. Will you get it down now, and tell Mr John that we start in twenty minutes."

How terrible all this was. There was William's voice calling for Robert. He was useless, that boy, quite useless. Why was he never there when he was wanted? He was a good riddance, worthless creature. And William was beginning to forget everything. What could one do?

They would have to take his box with them. And they would have to start earlier so as to have time to label it and everything. Really, John might have told them that he still had it in his room.

Ah, this sort of thing exhausted one. She was quite worn out. What with going through the village on a last round of visits and talking to everyone for the last time in one's official position, so to speak, one was worn out. Then she had given a farewell tea-party to the neighbours, a terrible affair. But they had said nice things on the Board of Guardians, and the Parish Council had presented her with an address, she would never forget that. Weston was going to Mrs Parks, only three miles away, which was a good thing, for the soil here suited him. Wait, there was Annie! She had not seen Annie. But what was the good, the poor thing was quite crazy? Crayshaw was going to take her on in his garden, so that she would be all right. It was good of him, he had the village at heart. She would send Annie ten shillings when she got to London. Mrs Lane, too, was only moving two miles away, which was because she wanted to be near Herbert, of course, as he was staying on here to keep the garden tidy, till someone came to buy it. The house was sure to be sold, it was so beautiful, and the garden was the best in twenty miles. With Weston, Mrs Parks would win all the prizes at the Norbury Flower Show. He was a good gardener, quite excellent with chrysanthemums.

It was stupid to forget that trunk. Why, he had been sitting on it when she went up. She looked at her watch, ten minutes more, they ought to be off. But no, not quite yet, perhaps.

It was nice of Edward, he must have understood how terrible leaving Barwood would be to her. Having a foothold up there made house-huntin' so much more comfortable. Goin' away was like leaving half one's life behind one, but then the boy would be so much happier. She would be able to look up Mrs Malinger, who used to live in Norbury years ago, she was such a nice woman.

Had she put in the medicine chest? There, she had forgotten. But perhaps it was in. She leapt up and hurried upstairs to her bedroom. Out of the window there was the view over the lawn. And there was the cock pheasant being cautious at the bottom there. He and his wives could eat all the bulbs now. That lawn, how beautiful it was. And in the wild garden at the side the daffodils were beginning to come out, such a mass of yellow. Well, they were going. What had she come here for, she had been round the garden yesterday? Yes, the medicine chest. She looked, and it was there still. She had forgotten. It must come up by the van. How stupid of her, for towns were so unhealthy and the boy might need a tonic. Oh dear, the garden. They ought to be off soon. She hurried downstairs again. There was William.

"The car is round, madam."

"Very well."

Wait a minute, just to show him she did not have train fever. But that was childish.

"John dear, get your coat on and come, or we shall have a rush at the station."

His voice from above:

"Coming."

"William, I entirely forgot about the medicine chest in my room. Will you send that on in the van."

"Yes, madam."

His voice, nearer:

"Coming."

"Are the suitcases in?"

"Yes, madam."

"Give me my coat, then."

"And, William, come and see us in London some time. Your brother is there, isn't he?"

"I will, madam, thank you."

Poor old thing, he was quite upset. It was rather terrible. Ah, here he was. How quickly he walked alone now.

"Be careful, dear."

"I'm all right."

"Well, let's get into the car. We have got plenty of time. Oh, William, the clock has stopped in the Hall there. I hope it isn't broken. You had better get Brown's man in to look to it."

They were off now. What did the clock matter as they weren't coming back, but they sold better if they were going. John was waving. No, she couldn't look back.

"So we are going?"

"Of course, dear."

He was so happy.

They were in the car on the way to the station, how extraordinary after so many weeks' work. Perhaps she had decided too quickly. Mabel, of course, had been right against it from the start. But the boy would only be happy in London, he wasn't made for the country, especially after he had gone blind like that. Only the other day and here they were. Oh, there was the Vicarage. How fast they were going.

"Hi! don't go so fast."

"I love speed."

"But it's so dangerous, dear."

"Where are we now?"

"In the sunken bit. He has slowed down, that's better. Dear boy, are you nearly enough wrapped up?"

Farther away, farther away. Everything had been leading up to this. The road went by with a swish, the rain made the surface so wet.

"Are you sure you haven't forgotten anythin'? There may be still time to go back."

"I don't think so."

There was the dove-cote. They were leaving so much behind. How fast the man drove. What was the good? But it was tiresome forgettin' John's box like that. It would put the excess luggage out, they would have to make a new bill, and that would take time. It would be a rush. There was Mrs Trench. She hadn't seen them, they were travellin' so fast. She was about to have another baby. There must be something in the family, it was the only way to account for all the Trench babies dying as soon just as they were born. It brought the average of infant mortality in the village so high.

"Where are we now?"

"Why are you so jumpy, dear? We are just going under the leanin' oak."

The leaning oak? There was a long way to go yet. The engine purred. London was the temple of machinery. It was hot in here.

"Shall we have a window down?"

"As you like. But it is rainin'."

The air came rushing in, sown with raindrops that spattered coolly against his face. He drank the wind in gulps, half-choking at the volume of it cramming down his throat. This was good. And the horn on this car had such an imperious note, but after all, great hopes were driving with it. They must go faster, faster, but then Mamma did not like it. The station was so far away, they might not catch their train. The horn again. He would like to take it away and have it in London as a souvenir to blow when things were not going well.

"Oh, John, look. There are the village."

"Which side?"

"There, to your left. Oh, you have missed them, they are behind now. How nice of them, how nice of them."

"Yes, that was nice of them."

"They were nearly all there. Oh dear."

"We shall come down and see them again soon."

"I saw Mrs Withers, and Mrs Hartley and old Mrs Eddy had come from the almshouses. I waved. They were waving. It would have been nice to stop, but we haven't the time."

"No, that would only have made a rush at the station."

Stopping like that would have been intolerable. Besides, it was better to break quickly with the old than to linger by it. The village would be all right. They must be on a hill now. How slow it was. They might miss that train. Then they could always take the next one. But it was this train that mattered, they must catch this train, he had thought so much of it, tearing across the country to the biggest town of all. Everything would give way to it, it was his train.

"We are just passing the last of your estate, dear"; for it was still his.

"Yes?"

Thank God for that. They were almost out of the circle now.

She did feel miserable, yes, it was being worse than she thought it would be. See how the corn was coming up, and the blossom just peeping through the trees. Two partridges, frightened by the car, shot away to curl over the hedge at the bottom of that field. Spring, and they were leaving. But then October was always the best month down here, they would come back for that, she had promised herself and Mabel. There was Norbury, quite close now, with some blue sky over it and a great rainbow, – over the station no doubt.

"Are you happy, John?"

"Yes, very."

What a fool of a man that was who was driving the cart. Why couldn't he get out of the way? That kind of labourer went to sleep, so the horses did too, of course. What was that? No. Yes, it was the Vincent boy on his motor bicycle. Mabel had been right, it was mad the pace he drove. Look at him – no, he was gone.

"Here we are in Norbury."

"Are we? Oh, well, it is not so very far now Yes, I can smell it. Splendid. What's the time?"

"We have another ten minutes yet. Look, there's the Tea Rooms, and Smith the boot shop, and Green the draper's."

The driver had turned out of the High Street. Only another minute. He could hardly sit still. That must be a coal dump they were passing. A train whistled. Joy. The car pulled up, he jumped out and then stood lost.

"Don't move a step without me, dear."

"All right."

"You might fall on to the rails or something. Where's Janet?"

That would indeed be an anti-climax.

"Here, John, come this way and sit on this seat."

How quiet it was here. A cursed sparrow was cheeping foolishly so near. The station seemed asleep. But he was going away. Behind in the waiting-room a voice droned on, while another laughed at intervals. There was Mamma's voice coming. She had got hold of Smith, poor man. He was being allowed to speak, "No trouble at all, Mrs Haye, at all. I will see to it immediately." She stopped by him.

"They are making out the excess luggage, my dear. I think it is all going to be all right."

"Good."

This seat was hideously hard. That sparrow. Why was no one moving? A burst of laughter from the waiting-room, there were quite a number of people in it. They would be travelling by the same train.

"Janet."

"Yes, Mr John."

"How much longer, Janet?"

"Only five minutes now."

Why did she speak as if he was a child? Here were steps coming towards him, boots clanking on the flags. The man had a smell of grease and leather about him.

"Porter?"

"Yessir."

"Is it a through train to London?"

"Change at Bridcote, Swindon and Oxford."

Why had Mamma not told him? So they were to travel provincially. Oh well. It was London, but it was not the express. They would crawl like a worm instead. Voices on all sides began to make themselves heard, growing louder and louder. Over them all was Mamma suddenly thanking Smith. Then she came and sat down by him.

"I have done it all, I think."

198

"Good."

"It will be in soon now."

"So we change three times."

"Yes, dear, do you mind? Such a nuisance. But it was the only train in the afternoon, and I thought we had better have lunch at home, it is so much more comfortable, don't you think?"

"Yes."

How funny that she had never consulted him. But she had always loved secrecy in her arrangements. A bell rang, steps began to make patterns of sound, and the voices rushed out of the waiting-room. They were off. A rumble which ran up to a roar and the train drew up. What a noise it was. But Mamma was dragging him along. A child's voice, plaintive, "Mumma . . . blind, Mumma." Yes, that was him.

"Here you are, dear, jump in. The corner seat. The carriage is reserved. I shall be back in a minute. Thank you, Smith. Now . . ."

So they were off. Good-bye. He had had so many. Where was Mamma? Oh, why didn't the train go?

CHAPTER IV

Beginning Again

London. He was sitting in the drawing-room of the house Uncle Edward had lent them. He was ill, ill. The sunlight streamed through the window by him, for it was spring, and ate stealthily into the plush which covered his armchair.

There was a sickly scent of flowers in the room. They had been sent up from Barwood and were fading, when once they had danced so wildly at the wind. The afternoon was heavy and the air thick with the sweetness of a dying lily just by him, a putrefaction drooping through the heat. The window was open and from beneath the noise of the street came in shafts, cutting through the steady sun. The ringing of bicycle bells shot up in necklaces of sound from the road, and jagged footsteps tore in upon his old life that was being left behind now with the song of that bird.

Oh, why had he gone blind? All these months now he had seen nothing, and he had pretended to others and even to himself that in feeling things he was as well off as one who saw them, but it was not true. For in London so much went on that there was no time to separate or analyse your sensations, everything crowded in upon you and left you dazed. But in a sense life was beginning again, for they would be so happy up here. In time he would learn to understand the streets. Mamma had found a house which would do, and soon they would be moving in. That would make another rift, for he would lose Margaret, the wife of the caretaker here. She had kept him alive, she was so vivid, and then sometimes she would dream, falling into long silences when her hand lay as if asleep in his. Probably she was hideous, but then he could not see. She must hate him with his scars.

The glass had ploughed through his face, as his blindness cut into his brain now, and they had taken him to the hospital where even the nurses had been antiseptic. Everything had felt most wickedly clean with a mathematical cleanness. But his nurse had had wonderful hands that hovered and that touched so lightly and yet helped when it hurt. Her fingers had been so lithe. It was silly to talk of "white mice" as he had with June, of how her fingers had scurried about in his; one needed strong unerring fingers. Margaret's were like that sometimes. But even the clean stench in that hospital had been better than this of the flowers, and anyway it had been quiet, not as here where these stabbing bursts of sound tortured you. But there was a whiff of tar in the air, and he liked tar.

Listen to that bird, singing as though there were nothing better to do in the world. Barwood was so far away now, yet, because he had seen there perhaps, he could not get away. The roar of the streets reminded one of the quiet which had been over it, where sounds came as if distilled by the great distances; and then Margaret was so different to June, June who had never known her place in the order of things – there was no place for her – and Margaret who knew her position exactly, and was so sure of herself. Why had that bird chosen this house on which to sing, little inconsequent notes being flung at the blue sky, crystal notes that shattered against the tawdriness of these dying flowers and of his own discontent? A car bore down and overwhelmed the song, but it emerged once more as the car sped away and made him ask if he had done right, to leave June like that, and to take Mamma away. For the garden at Barwood would be bursting into life just now, all the birds would be singing, and if Mamma were there she would be spying over the border and endlessly conferring with Weston. He would have been able to share in the spring as well, lying on the lawn in a chair he would have passed hours feeling the leaves come out and everything changing round him, while he was out of it in London, too lost, too tired to raise his head above the clatter of the streets, where everyone except himself had work to do. He must work.

He would write. At Noat he had thought about it, at Barwood he had talked about it, but he must work at it up here, there was nothing else to do, as he was left alone for hours, they were all so busy. In time he could get to understand the streets and so to write about them, for in time one would know more about them than people ever would who had sight. It was so easy to see and so hard to feel what was going on, but it was the feeling it that mattered. A bell rang downstairs. Someone was at the front door, coming to see him, perhaps; and then there was Mamma's voice with a shy laugh in it, saying:

"Why, it's Lorna! My dear, I recognised you at once. How nice of you! Just think, you after these years and years. I happened to be passing so I opened."

And a strange voice was talking at the same time, then they both kissed – why need Mamma kiss so loudly in London? – and the strange voice rose over Mamma's and was saying:

"Emily – such ages and ages . . ."

But a motor bike passed and cut them off from him, he only heard the front door crash as they shut it. Someone to see Mamma, well, that would make her very happy. But he was forgotten up here, he was only allowed the echoes of all that was going on, and he saw himself waiting and listening here for the rest of his life. No one cared whether he was blind or not. But there were steps outside, it was Margaret, she minded, and he would fascinate her so that she minded all the more. There was a knock on the door, her knock, and she slipped in on a gust of cool air from the marble hall, and there was something cool about her as

202

well, waves of gentleness breaking round him. Every time she came he was surprised at her quietness. She was so deft, but then she had been a lady's-maid. Her skirt touched his foot so lightly.

"I'm just going out, Mr Haye, and I thought I'd look in to see if I could find you anything."

"Take me out."

"Mrs Haye just said she would do that herself, she won't be long now."

To be taken out! He was in everyone's way. And why shouldn't he go with Margaret? Now he would have to wait till that visitor had gone.

"Are you comfortable in that chair, Mr Haye?" and her hand arranged the handkerchief in his breast pocket. She was listless to-day, her thoughts were elsewhere. And she had scented herself, the first time she had ever done that since he had known her. It was very, very faint, but you could just tell it if you were near her. Perhaps it was meant for someone who would be nearer. He would be. He searched round his handkerchief for her hand.

"But your hand is burning. Well, I never," and hers had escaped; "I must be going."

"Could you pull the blind down and shut the window, the noise is so frightful?"

The blind ran down and he thought of how to detain her. The window shut and the world became muffled.

"Oh, and this lily here, could you move it?"

She tugged, but the stand that held it was heavy, and her breathing grew deeper at the effort.

"Let me help. There is nothing in the way, is there?"

"I can do it; don't get up, Mr Haye."

But he was on his feet and groping about when he met her hand again, calm and a trifle moist, which took his and guided it. His other hand meeting her shoulder slid down the dress (through which her arm glowed) till his fingers caught on her elbow. How small it was, but it wriggled,

203

and seized with a sudden despair he loosed it. Then, as he was groping forward again, the lily poked gently into his face, trying to tickle him, and shuddering, he pushed the thing away. He leant forward further to where he felt her presence and the stand. Her breath burned in his face for a moment and bathing in her nearness he leant further forward still, in the hopes of finding her, but she dropped his hand and it fell on the slick edges of the pot in which the lily grew. Despair was coming over him again, it was too awkward, this pursuit of her under a lily, when all at once her arm mysteriously came up over his mouth, glowing and cool at the same time, and the scent was immediately stronger, tangible almost, so that he wanted to bite it. But before he could do that her arm had glided away again and he gave it up, and was merely irritated when a stray bit of her hair tickled his right cheek, so different to the lily, as they were pushing the stand away. But when they had the thing moved and she was leading him back, he felt so glad at the touch of her presence that once again he could not bear the thought of her going.

"Don't leave me. Sit here for a little, I am so continually alone."

"I must go, really, I shall be late already. My brother's come up for the day and I'm to meet him. Is there anything else you want?"

Her brother. It was no good, there was someone else, just as June would have someone else now. How could they like him with his scars? He raised a hand and slipped the fingers along them, smooth varnished things unlike the clinging life of his skin. The door shut, she was gone, and the coolness with her. He was alone. That child on the platform as they had been coming up here: "Look, Mumma, . . . blind, Mumma," and the horror which had been in its little cursed treble because another little thing had thrown a stone at a passing train. Of course it had been his window the stone hit, of course. A motor horn kept on braying in the street outside. And now that the blind was down and that the window was shut he felt that he would suffocate, and that those flowers were watching him and mocking because they could do something that he could not.

He must go out, but he must wait first for Mamma as he could not find his way about. Their walks were terrifying very often, crossing a street Mamma would lose her head, pulling on his arm this way and that while death in a car rushed down on them and passed in a swirl, gathering the air after it, and all the time he was trying not to show how frightened he was. Then, when they were on the pavement at last, people had no mercy on you if it was crowded; you were always being jostled, and broken ends of conversation were jumbled up and thrown at you, and then presences would glide past leaving a snatch of warm scent behind them to tantalise. He was continually running into dogs, he trod on them, and they howled till their owners became angry and then apologised when they realised that you were not as others were. In the country you had been able to forget that you were blind.

Everything was pressing down on him to-day, crowding in on him, dragging him down. And now that the window was shut and the sun cut off by the blind he felt suffocated. A barrel-organ was thudding a tune through the window, beating at the threshold of his brain. He got up and groping towards the window opened it. As he did so there was a sudden lull in all the noise, he could only hear the clop-clop of a horse receding into the distance, and then mysteriously from below there floated up a chuckle; it was a woman and someone must have been making love to her, so low, so deep it was. He was on fire at once. Love in the street, he would write of it, love shouting over the traffic, unsettling the policemen, sweeping over the park, wave upon wave of it, inciting the baboons to mutiny in the Zoo, clearing the streets. What was the use of his going blind if he did not write? People must hear of what he felt, of how he knew things differently. The sun throbbed in his head. Yes, all that, he would write all that. He was on the crest of a petulant wave, surging along, when his wave broke on the sound of a motor horn. There were his scars, and the sun pricked at him through them. He drew back into the room, his face wet with the heat. Oh, he was tired.

As he searched for his chair a flower poked its head confidingly into his open hand, but he crushed it, for what had he to do with flowers now? Why did Mamma leave him alone, a prey to all his thoughts? They must go out, Mamma and he, but he felt so ill. And was she happy here, away from Barwood and all the worries that she had lived for? As for him, it was only that he was dazed by all these new sensations, he would rise above them soon, when he knew how to interpret them, and then he would have some peace.

A car was pulled up sharp, the brakes screamed and he writhed at it. He was imprisoned here, for somehow he could not learn to find his way about in this new house. Why didn't she come?

It was hot. It made him think of Barwood, where probably it would be raining, and of sitting in the summer-house while the cool rain spattered softly in washing away the scars, and where the wind brought things from afar to hang for a moment in his ears and then take away again. Years ago the trees there had been green for him, only months ago really, and here there was only dust and the dying flowers and tar. And he had fished where the sunset came to earth and bathed in the river. But there were voices coming up the stairs, Mamma's and a new voice. They must be glad to be together again, because the two streams of what they had to say to each other mingled as they both talked at the same time and purled so happily on. The door opened. He got up shyly.

"Who have you brought?"

"My dear, what do you think, it is Lorna Greene. Just think, we had not met since I married. Oh, Lorna, this is like old days."

She was so excited and laughing, she must be happy. Then her voice dropped. "Lorna, this is John." All the life had gone out of her voice, but then why wonder at it, after all he was the problem and the millstone. Damn them! But he was saying:

"Oh, how do you do," while a strange hand, languid but interested, took his for a moment and he felt many rings and much culture. He had never in his life held anything so cared for, she must bathe this hand in oil every night, it was so smooth, so impersonal. Then it coolly slipped away again, and she was saying something about his having known her son at Noat in an amused kind of drawl, her voice curling round her lips. It was almost as if she were laughing at him. She searched with her voice, it was sardonic, she would drive him mad. What was there funny about him, except that he was stuck here defenceless?

"Lorna, my dear, I can't hear myself speak. These appallin' motors and things don't give me a minute's peace. Why don't the police do somethin' about it? It is nice to have you here. I am shuttin' the window, John, do you mind?"

No, he didn't mind. Window shut, window open, you were boxed up just the same. They sat down, talking hard. Very long ago he remembered this woman at Noat, Greene's mother, she had been tall and he had thought her nondescript. And now there was so much in her voice and in her hand. In this way one gained by being blind. But she was talking and her voice was fascinating.

"Do you remember when I was staying with you that time, Emily, and the minister came to tea, the yearly tea your father gave him? And how we put mustard into all the cakes he was fondest of, and he noticed nothing and ate them all, then stayed talking longer than he had ever done before, all about how the family were like the cedar in front of the house?"

"And what Solomon's temple was made of . . ."

They were remembering, they all did.

"And oh, Lorna, do you remember . . ."

Mamma's voice was quite different, as if it had suddenly leapt into youth again, it was so happy and excited. So London was a success with her, she was really enjoying herself for the first time! There was only himself out of it, all the others were in the swim.

"And, Emily, when we fed the dog on chocolate and it was sick all over your father's room, how furious he was!"

Oh, naughty, naughty! This happiness of theirs was exasperating. How ludicrous to think that, but he could not help it. And then all the time this Greene woman was speaking she seemed to be gibing at him. They had no life, they lived only in what was passed, while June and he had carved great slices out of the future when they had been together. June, at any rate, had always been there ready to come when she was wanted, but Margaret's time was divided. Why couldn't Mamma and he go out for their walk, but then she was so happy talking. There was no air now that they had shut the window, they had muffled the room so that they might muffle him the better with this talk of theirs. On and on it went, dragging one back just when one was beginning to strike out into new ground. He must plunge into the tumult outside and find a place for himself. He got up.

"It is so hot in here, do you mind if I open the window?"

"Let me do it for you."

"No, no, I can do it."

Why couldn't they leave him alone? Of course he could do it, he was not wholly incapacitated. Where was the catch? He must look such a fool fumbling here.

Good heavens! the boy looked ghastly. Why hadn't she noticed before, it was Lorna's having come that had excited her so that she had not seen. And as she helped him raise the sash she looked anxiously into his face, she did not like it, he seemed from his expression to be seeing things which she could not. But then how could he? He was not going to be ill? She blamed herself, how selfish of her to be gossiping with Lorna when he was ill and needed her. All this noise must be bad for him with the window open, but then it was air he wanted, and it was rather sticky to-day. Lorna must go. But it was as if the dear thing had guessed, for she was saying that she must fly now and that she knew her way and that no one was to show her out. But you couldn't do that, Edward had left no servants, and as they went downstairs Lorna was told how the journey up a few weeks before had made the boy unaccountably seedy, how at first the noise seemed to worry him terribly, but that the new house would be quieter, and how worrying it all was. What could one do?

The soft sound of their murmuring at the bottom of the stairs and the roar of Oxford Street swept him away on a flood, but he was so tired that he seemed to sink in it to a place where the pitch was higher, the cars and everything more shrill as they darted along so far away, it seemed. The flowers were singing to themselves, or was it a bird? Birds lusting in trees which suddenly were round him, their notes screaming through the rich leaves. They were full of sap, hanging down thick hands to cover the nakedness of the branches on which birds sat mocking at him, for they could see and he could not. All Barwood was laughing at him because he had gone away, and by doing that had found out how helpless he was. He could not open the window, he could not go out.

Mamma was coming back, her footsteps rang heavily on the stairs, and as she came in and shut the door he roused himself, saying that he was only feverish and that it would pass with a night's rest. She came up to him and laid her hand on his shoulder.

"Are you all right, dear?"

"Yes, yes, quite all right."

Why did they go on nagging him?

"Shall I shut the window? Don't you find this noise terrible?"

"No, please leave it open so that I can listen." She sat down and took up some knitting. That doctor was a fool. What was the matter with the boy? She could only sit and watch, there was nothing to be done with him, he was in one of his moods. Their walk was out of the question now.

He passed a hand over his forehead, the skin was dry and burning, electric. Again he felt that he was being enveloped, this time by the close room and by the sun which throbbed outside. He was growing afraid at the way in which the walls pressed in and crowded the flowers together so that their scent rose up in a fog mixed with the turmoil outside and made to overwhelm him, when suddenly and for no reason, like a gust of wind through the room, purifying it, came the sound of bells from the church along the street, tearing through the room, bells catching each other up, tripping, tumbling and then starting off again in cascades. Theirs was such a wild joy and they trembled at it between the strokes so that they hummed, making a background for the peals. He loved bells and, inexpressibly happy, he was swept back to Barwood and June – "Listen, June, how the sound of them comes over the country," and her father being hunted by them through the mazes that gin had created in his brain, and their walks stretched in a gesture to the sky, they had been so unfortunate in their lives.

Then, for no reason, the bells began to stop one by one and the humming grew fainter, and he remembered an evening on the river when the sound of them had glided over the water, but a lorry mumbled along beneath, and one by one the bells stopped till even their humming had gone. Barwood was being sold, and after all, those walks of theirs had come to nothing.

He must ask B. G. and Seymour round to see him. But

perhaps they would be bored and would laugh at his ideas after the time they had spent at Oxford. And he was not going to let them see him crushed under his blindness, they would despise him for it. He must first make out how he stood with life in general so that he could show them how much better off he was than they. He would start a crusade against people who had eyesight. It was the easiest thing in the world to see, and so very many were content with only the superficial appearance of things; it would teach them so much if they were to go blind, though blindness was a burden at first and he was heavy with memories.

Those bells, everything, brought them jostling back in one's mind. But there had been something different about the bells, they had left him trembling, and when he passed a hand over his chair he was surprised at how stolid and unaltered the plush remained, for he was certain that the wild peal of them had made a great difference, their vibration had loosened and freed everything, until even the noise of the streets became invigorating. He felt a stirring inside him; it was true, they had made a difference, he felt it, and in a minute something was going to happen. He waited, taut, in the chair.

Mrs Haye knitted. The bells carried one back to Barwood. He would have been better there, you could not breathe in London, and fresh air was good for one if one was feelin' seedy. But it was no use thinkin' about Barwood, one must be practical, and everything would change once they had a house of their own. This caretaker and his wife were impossible, it was so like Edward to have servants like that. You could not speak to the man he was so rude, and that woman was hardly any better, though she did seem to take some trouble with the boy. But there again you never quite knew, he might form one of his terrible attachments for her, and then there would be the old worry of the Entwhistle creature all over again. She ought to have stood up to him at the time and told him straight out that it was

ridiculous and that she would not have it, it was wrong of
her not to have done that, but then his blindness had come
upon them so suddenly and it had been so soon after. You
could not speak out to him when his life had been taken
from him like that. Anyway, they had gone and it was done
– so much of her was there, in the village and the Town
Council and all those things, but of course one understood
his wanting to get away from all the old places where he
had seen, and he was so brave making a new life for himself
like this. And she would make a home for him, they would
start again up here, it was rather excitin' really, of course it
was. She would get hold of Lorna and they would find
some young things. He must marry. If he did, perhaps she
could go back there?

Lorna had altered, she was so fashionable now, one felt
shy meetin' her again. It had been good of her to come
round, she was goin' to be a real help, for they must find
something to distract the boy. She had bought that lily, one
would have thought he'd like it, it had cost quite a sum
being so early in the year, but he had pushed it away. Better
not to mention that. These motor cars, it was a disgrace the
noise they made. But he seemed to like it, for he was lookin'
happy almost for the first time since he had been up here.
He had said all the time that he was very happy, but she
had felt that he had been worried really, and mainly as to
whether she was happy in London, but of course she went
where he went. It was difficult to understand his moods.
Perhaps they could go for their walk now, and that she had
only been imaginin' things when she thought he was ill.

Oh, these waves of sickness that came suddenly over
him, stirring through his brain. And it was as if there were
something straining behind his eyeballs to get out. He
dropped his face into his hands, there was such a feeling of
happiness surging through him.

Mamma's voice, a long way away it seemed, and anxious:
"What is it, dear?"

"I'm frightened."

"Why? What is there to be frightened of? Why?"

But he was frightened at such joy. In a minute he felt it would burst out of him in a great wind and like a kite he would soar on it, and that the mist which lay between him and the world would be lifted by it also. Rising, rising up.

He was rising through the mist, blown on a gust of love, lifting up, straining at a white light that he would bathe in. He half rose.

"John!"

And when he bathed there he would know all, why he was blind, why life had been so to him. He was nearer. To rise on this love, how wonderful to rise on this love. He was near now.

"John!!"

A ladder, bring a ladder. In his ears his own voice cried loudly, and a deeper blindness closed in upon him.

★　　★　　★

As they carried him to his room, the bells suddenly broke out again from along the street. Probably they were practising for some great event. It was the first thing he heard as he came back to the world, and he smiled at them.

A LETTER

"Dear B. G.

"They tell me I have had some sort of a fit, but it has passed now. Apparently my father was liable to them, so that anyway I have one behind me after this. But it is so divine to be in London again near to you, and with the sun shining down on me as I lie in bed as if it had never shone before, while underneath, in the street, the traffic glides past in busy vibrations, I am so happy to be in the centre of things again, and to be alive. How stimulating a town is — but perhaps you think me silly. You have led such a different life to mine, I hardly know what you think or feel. Come round and look me up again, you know how I love talking. I have had a wonderful experience. I am going to settle down to writing now, I have a lot to tell. Mamma read me your article in the 'New World' and it was wonderful — really, I mean, for that is not flattery. Why am I so happy to-day?

"Yrs.,
"John."

Other novels by Henry Green published in Harvill Paperback

LIVING

"The masterpiece of this disciplined, poetic and grimly realistic, witty and melancholy, amorous and austere voluptuary"
ROSAMOND LEHMANN

"The best novel of working-class life we have"
WALTER ALLEN

CAUGHT

"This is Mr Green's best book . . . Must be read by anyone who claims a serious interest in the novel"
ALAN PRYCE-JONES

"Should be read by anyone who believes that the English novel has died a natural death"
PHILIP TOYNBEE

LOVING

"Green's best-known and possibly best novel"
JOHN UPDIKE

"A work of art of mischievous brilliance and eccentricity . . . As light and round and flawless as a bubble . . . It mirrors the world with a richness and a fullness that dazzle the beholder"
New Yorker

NOTHING

"This brilliant and subtle book is entirely enjoyable and very funny"
STEVIE SMITH

"An amusing, brittle, sensible comedy of parents and children, displaying the gulf between the prudishness of the younger generation and the flightiness of their elders"
PAMELA HANSFORD JOHNSON

Harvill Paperbacks are published by
The Harvill Press

For the full list of titles please write to:

The Harvill Press,
84 Thornhill Road, London N1 1RD
enclosing a stamped self-addressed envelope